Books written by the author as Erasmus Cromwell-Smith II

In English	En español
THE EQUILIBRIST SERIES	LA SERIE EL EQUILIBRISTA
(INSPIRATIONAL/PHILOSOPHICAL)	(INSPIRACIONAL/FILOSÓFICO)
The Happiness Triangle (Vol. 1)	El triángulo de la felicidad (Vol. 1)
Geniality (Vol. 2)	Genialidad (Vol. 2)
The Magic in Life (Vol. 3)	La magia de la vida (Vol. 3)
Poetry in Equilibrium (Vol. 4)	Poesía en equilibrio (Vol. 4)
The Orloj Series	La serie El Orloj
(YOUNG ADULTS)	(JÓVENES ADULTOS)
The Orloj of Prague (Vol. 1)	El Orloj de Praga (Vol. 1)
The Orloj of Venice (Vol. 2)	El Orloj de Venecia (Vol. 2)
The Orloj of Paris (Vol. 3)	El Orloj de Paris (Vol. 3)
The Orloj of London (Vol. 4)	El Orloj de Londres (Vol. 4)
Poetry in Balance (Vol. 5)	Poesía en Balance (Vol. 5)

The South Beach Conversational method (Educational)	EL MÉTODO CONVERSACIONAL SOUTH BEACH (Educacional)
• Spanish	• Inglés,
• German	• Alemán
• French	• Francés
• Italian	• Italiano
• Portuguese	• Portugués

The Nicolas Tosh Series
(Sci-fi)
Algoritm-323 (Vol. 1)
Tosh (Vol. 2)

As Nelson Hamel*

THE PARADISE ISLAND SERIES	THE RB HACKERS SERIES
(Action/Thriller)	(Sci/fi)
Miami Beach, Dangerous Lifestyles (Vol. 1)	*White Spaces at Lake Erie* (Vol.1)

* In collaboration with Charles Sibley.

All titles are or will be available in audiobook

Poetry in Equilibrium

The Equilibrist series: Vol. IV

Erasmus Cromwell-Smith II

Poetry in Equilibrium
© Erasmus Cromwell-Smith II
© Erasmus Press
This is a work of fiction. Names, characters, businesses, places, events, and incidents are either the products of the author's imagination or used in a fictitious manner. Any resemblance to actual persons, living or dead, or actual events is purely coincidental.
All rights reserved. No part of this book may be reproduced in any form or by any electronic or mechanical means, without permission in writing from the Copyright owner.
ISBN: 978-1-7330289-3-6
Library of Congress Case Number: 1-8614878641
Publisher: RCHC LLC
Editor: Elisa Arraiz Lucca
Proof-reading: Charles Sibley, Janet Bartos, D. Suster, Tracy Ann-Wynter
Cover Design, and Interior Design: Alfredo Sainz
erasmuscromwellsmith.com Second edition
Printed in USA, 2022

Note by The Author,

The story behind the creation of the second and third volumes of The Equilibrist series:

While writing The Equilibrist series, my intent has been to craft artful verses that are straightforward, easy to understand. The emphasis has been on the message, not on getting the reader lost in the traditional intricacies, metrics even incomprehensible abstractions of traditional poetry. Through art that speaks to all, I seek to elicit emotions while provoking reflection. Verses that jump with ease out of the pages of a book, enrapturing anyone's heart. By writing free verse as if it was a meaningful conversation among friends, I've aimed to break the common apathy or predisposition towards poetry in general. On every theme, I asked myself many times over, the following questions:

- Am I passionate enough about this subject matter?
- Is my vision on the subject somehow different than the norm?
- Can I articulate it through art?
- Have I educated myself sufficiently about each particular source of inspiration?
- Can I write something that could be interpreted and experienced in different dimensions?
- Can I compose versatile poetry that is as light or as deep as the reader may want it to be?
- Can I create a verse that inspires, impacts, even heals others?

If the answers to all these questions were affirmative, I embarked into meditative and introspective journeys searching for the next magic creative moment. From then on, visualization coupled with sensing of the subject matter unleashed torrents of words that became a poem, a fable, an essay, or a scribble.

The poetry of The Equilibrist series draws a circle of life, covering existential ground that brings along, inspirational, emotional, and spiritual enrichment to an otherwise mundane life. "Poetry in Equilibrium" is dedicated to all those poetry lovers that want to experience the trilogy's prose without a storyline or a plot framing it. As a special treat, at the end of the book, I've included a short play, which is very close to my heart. It's called "No Longer Just a Dream." Additionally, I've incorporated detailed notes at the back of the book. They reflect what I was feeling when I wrote each verse, essay, scribble, or fable. I sincerely hope you enjoy "Poetry in Equilibrium" as much as I did when creating it.

Erasmus Cromwell-Smith II.

"The Quibbler and The Street Juggler"

Standing by the corner under the broken streetlamp,
on a dusky, foggy & misty night,
The Quibbler does what he always does,
He mumbles & grumbles, rambles & tumbles
his thoughts & words
about anyone and anything.

His big blue eyes dart in near darkness,
right & left, left & right.
And they seem,
while filled with magnetic intensity,
as if about to pop out, of his eye sockets!

And as he stares,
trying to follow the pirouettes of the lonely shadow,
he wonders aloud,

"What is it with this fellow?"

Down the street, unaware of being watched,
he juggles while sitting high above the cobblestones,
pedaling the single wheel in quick bursts,
while glued to the saddle,
contorting into impossible angles and acrobatic circles,
always defying gravity,
backwards, downwards, upwards & sideways.

He juggles while in balance,
his hands are always
keeping multiple objects floating in the air,
but never handling more than two at once.
Despite the swings, twists & turns,
he never loses focus nor concentration, and does it all
with absolute confidence, and resolute determination.

"Yeah, yeah, yeah, but why juggle?" The Quibbler rambles non-stop.
"And so, what?"
"Who cares about living a life on the edge, filled with contortions
and near misses in every corner?"

"Because that's what we do in life,
we juggle & seek to maintain balance,
and through practice & experience
we want to master both as he does,
as if they were second nature to us."

Finally, reason prevails & The Quibbler concludes,
"As the Juggler, again & again,
we strive & we struggle through the streets of life,
sometimes by defying the impossible & the improbable.
That's what we do,
we seek, we find & we conquer, then hang on for dear life."

"To maintain balance and be a master Juggler,
requires a disciplined & constant effort,
as they are both a couple of the keys,
to a wholesome & well-grounded life."

"The Equilibrist"

Our lives are like those of circus equilibrists,
we walk through a thin & narrow, but very strong wire,
our emotional life.

The wire is our support system,
made out of thousands of filaments tightly wound together.

Along it lie, among others,
our feelings, our faith, our friends & family.

Equilibrium is tough and challenging,
as it requires endless focus, rehearsal, and attention.

Just as the wire does, life swings,
up & down & right & left.

As the tightrope walker slides each slipper forward,
as if caressing the wire,
his feat as our lives, becomes a balancing act.

The more he, like us, practices equilibrium,
the more knowledge & experience he acquires,
the more self-confident he becomes,
because a man on a wire requires near perfection
on each of his well-choreographed moves.

Without a solid emotional life supporting us,
like the wire of an equilibrist,
there is no balance in life.

When we fall into excesses of effort (like work),
or excesses of discharge (like fun),
we lose equilibrium and fall from the wire.

And the safety nets down under, if we have them,
become our life savers.

When supported by the wire,
and if we attain sound self-confidence,
we can walk unaided
through the swings of life.

But the ultimate balance
is only attained by the equilibrist, with the stick,
which is love.

"The Balloon Salesman"

The young man with the tam-o'-shanter wanders around the park,
a cloud of Balloons follows him wherever he goes,
and one by one the small children come and go away,
with their Balloons softly tied to their little fingers.

"Balloons, Balloons for sale!" "I sell them for a bargain."
"I've got Reds, Blues and Yellows."

"Round, Tear Drop or Heart-Shaped."
"Just pick one and this may be your Lucky day!"

The whisper of a voice comes from nowhere,
The Balloon salesman twists and turns to face his small customer.
He is flustered,
as his sudden move tangles the lines and Balloons above him.

The child stares at the salesman, arms crossed,
slightly tilted head & the pose of a quite amused
but still potentially good client.

"How can I help you, Sir?" "Why do you sell Balloons?"
As he untangles himself, he gazes benignly at his inquisitor.

"That's a very good question, young man."
"Actually, what I sell are Dreams."
"Dreams?"
"Well, as people grow older
they either lose their ability or desire to Dream,
so it's easy to buy one from me."

"But I do not see any adults buying Balloons."
"That's right, only children like you
seem to have an interest, let alone pay,
to walk away with their Dreams,
tied in a knot around their fingers,
floating above their heads wherever they go."

"Why do we Dream?"
"To chase our truest wishes and desires."

He frees up all his Balloons into a tight formation above him
and is finally able to face his diminutive interrogator,
who has not moved from his wide stance even one inch.

"But very few kids ask as many questions as you do.
Tell you what kid:
Today is your Lucky Day!"
"Your curiosity is about to open new doors for you,
I will take you for a ride
into the World of Dreams and the Land of Imagination."

Then a giant Balloon, with the colors of a Rainbow,
softly lifts them up into the open skies,
and drifts slowly towards the endless Horizon.

"When we Dream, we float above reality.
From a Balloon the fields look greener, the trees seem lusher,
the buildings & the streets appear neatly organized,
and the lakes & the rivers seem like the blood vessels of nature,
because as we hover, everything moves slowly underneath,
allowing us to see & better appreciate the details in life."

"As in a Dream, there is no direction in a Balloon flight,
hence we journey without a destination
and that in turn provides us with absolute freedom,
that's because we have no constrains & feel unfiltered.
When we Dream, we see the truth about ourselves,
and visualize, wish & think about life & people,
the way we really feel about them."

"When we float above reality, we're also able to see
The Magnificence of Life, The Perfection of Nature,
and The Harmony and Sheer Magnitude of the Universe."

Slowly, the giant Balloon descends back to reality.
Then, the Balloon salesman ties a big one with bright and shiny colors

to his middle finger,
and the child walks away happy with his Dreams floating above him.

"Balloons, Balloons for sale!" "I sell them cheap!"
"I've got Reds, Blues & Yellows."
"Just pick one & this may be your Lucky Day!"

"The Boy in The Picture"

The boy leans forward with his hands on the soil,
his legs bent, his feet off the ground
except for his tippy toes.
He is ready to bolt like a sprinter.

But his head tells a different story.
With his neck overextended, tilted to one side,
he gazes in the distance.
Is it an intense stare?
Is he just observing attentively?
No. His body denotes nerves.

His body exhibits tension while his head exudes calmness.
One body, two tales.

He is actually peeking, that's what he is doing.
He does not want to be seen
as he is watching something he is not supposed to.
Something he's been told countless times not to.
And yet, he still goes and does it anyhow.

So, what is he doing...? He dreams.
He dreams through the intense lights
coming out of the barn in the distance.

His neighbor, a funny looking and sounding hermit,
builds homemade rockets and sends them high up into the sky.

The boy dreams about the magician farmer
that makes the impossible and improbable real.
He wonders at his stubborn & sheer determination,
in spite of his rockets failing again and again.

The boy marvels at his creativity and unlimited energy.
'That's what I want to be,' he reasons.
'I want to reach the stars, the planets.
I want to fly into space & the universe.

'Through him I've learned that anything is possible,
even though at home I am told is not,
even if I am forbidden to watch,
even if those close to me don't know what it is to dream.'

The boy leans forward even more,
He visualizes the life ahead of him,
He is already living in the future.
He knows what he wants,
He knows where he is going.

And his journey begins right there, kneeling on a dirt field,
while peeking at a forbidden rocket factory in a barn
of an unlikely farmer-rocketeer.
It begins with an improbable and seemingly impossible dream
from a boy in a picture.

"The Gift of life"

When you hear the whispers of sorrow,
counter them with dreams of tomorrow.

When you feel the trappings of failure,
fight them with the thrills & excitement of being alive.

When you feel emptiness & solitude,
counter them with your heart and faith.

When you find yourself in the jaws of defeat,
push it back with conviction & grit.

When you feel zapped and exhausted,
tumble it by recharging and recovering with zeal.

When you feel consumed by poisonous anger,
dissipate it with grace and forgiveness.

When you feel trapped and without options in life's endless labyrinths,
conquer it by turning around and around, looking, and searching,
but never, ever, giving up, until you find one.

And when you've defied life in such ways,
always remember that such feats, are always,
What is expected of you?
What is required of you?
Since you were given "the gift of life" By God.

"The Unwavering, Unflickering, Tiny, Little Flame"

At the very deep ends of my heart,
in a place where emotions are raw,
where feelings are unedited,
At Love's nest and launching pad,
And where passions reign free,
With indomitable force,
Lies this Unwavering, "Unflickering"
Tiny, Little Flame that simply,
won't go away, won't quit, won't die.

It just continues to burn and churn, steadily and stubbornly,
with overwhelming heat and unstoppable intensity,
No matter What, No matter When.

Its serene hues of blue and yellow are stunningly beautiful,
Its blinding reds and oranges are awesome and powerful.

Thus, I ask myself,
What is life without our Tiny Little Flame?

What are we without it?
Well, we either are or live
a Life in Black and White or one in Full Technicolor,
with our inner fire endlessly burning within.

At the very deep ends of my heart,
filled with Feelings, Emotions, Passions, and Love,
lies this Unwavering, "Unflickering"
Tiny, Little Flame, that simply,
Won't go away,
No matter what, no matter when,
It simply won't quit,
It simply won't die,
It never waivers,
It never flickers,
It never ends.

"The Magic in Life"

What is it?
Is it just light that filters and flows through everything?
or colors and tones that paint it all?
Or the forces of nature,
sometimes sleeping giants, some others, roaring thunder.

And where is it?
Is it in the overwhelming scenery of the high mountains?
Is it in the translucent green of the tropical seas?
Or in the serene beauty of flowers?

Is it in the sun exploding in thousands of red colors
as it sets in the horizon?
Or the moon shining through the night sky
in endless shade of white?

Is it just to gaze at the innocent smile of a child?
or the little doggie wagging his tail?
or the loving eyes of a mother?
or into the countless stories and wisdom of grandma?
or is it about the family sitting at the table,
laughing, arguing, and sharing after a meal?

Or is it just being here…?

And where does it lie?
Is it only in the simple things? or does it lie in kindness?
Does it lie in passion, happiness, or equilibrium?

Is it in the exhilarating high of winning?
Or in the deflating low of losing?

Is it in the passionate enjoyment of competitive sports?
or in the quiet solitude of extraordinary individual efforts?

Is it in the majestic flight of an eagle?
or in the indestructible frame of an elephant?
or on the outer space sounds of a whale?
or the deadly jaws of a croc?
Is it in the endless beauty of a piece of art?
or in the dazzling fantasy of a great movie?
Is it in the guilty pleasure of a magnificent meal?
or in the feast to the senses of an endless tune?

Is it within the silence and peace of contemplation and meditation?
or in the never-ending enrichment of spirit & soul though faith?

Or is it in our ability to distort mundane reality?

Is it in the world of <u>dreams, fantasies, and imagination</u>
of those who dare and risk to?
or in the world of creators, inventors and tinkerers
that turn <u>them</u> into art, products, and crafts?

How about in the contagious ingenuity of endless hope?
or in the disarming innocence of unstoppable enthusiasm?

Or the passing moments of true and genuine happiness
when the trumpets of Heaven play our "Echoes of Life,"

Or is it in the atonement of our faults and errors
through the power of forgiveness and humility?

Or is it simply in the smile of one
who wakes up every day happy and thankful to be alive?

Or is it in the all-embracing clash
between endless passion and flesh?

Or is it simply when you are truly in love,
and your heart does not belong to you.

Where is it then?
This enchanted life God's given to us.

What is it then?
This magic spell that gives us the privilege of being alive.

The answer is in all of the above, and much, much more.

Because there is never ending and endless joy,
every second we are alive!
The answer lies within us and is self-evident.
The Magic in Life is everywhere!
and in everything around us!

And in order to capture it
You only have to Love Life!
as it is being given to you,
by God.

"The Blue Unicorn"

Wizard, Wizard!
Bring me a Blue Unicorn,
one that sprinkles Magic into Life,
innocence and candor to the spirit,
light, and color to the soul,
passion and love into one's heart,
meaning and purpose
for each and every day we are alive.

And in a snap! I am staring at my dream,
In awe and wonder I contemplate my fantasy.

Let a spell be cast, Wizard!
Let me have a Unicorn,
Let it be Blue as the Clearest of all Skies,
And Let it be Strong
as to conjure all the Forces of the Universe.

On my Unicorn I want to ride through life,
on an Endless Journey,
Around and Around,
And make of the Ups and Downs,
a Merry-Go-Around"
of effortless and well-lived circles.

Wizard, wizard,
Bring me a Blue Unicorn,
one of those that makes life a Magic Carpet Ride,
one that makes it all worthwhile.

"A Song in The Rain"

Today I woke up staring at a choice, feeling inspired,
I recalled how difficult it is been
to arrive at such crossroads.

Is happiness a choice? I've asked myself,
again and again, again and again.

In the end, the answer lies
in the most unexpected of places,
a Song in the Rain.

The Music notes feel wet, awash by the downpour.

And yet,
The Music quietly irrupts and pushes its way through.

The song comes through the rain,
The Tune and The Melody deafen the sound of the rain drops.

I can hear the music everywhere, as the sky drums like a waterfall.

And yet,
Nothing! Can stop the beauty and the power
of a Song in The Rain.

"Way, Way Up There"

Way, way up there
Where one can almost touch the sky,
well beyond the horizon,
there's an endless rainbow,
filled with extraordinary colors,
so bright and so shiny,
that they are a feast to the eye beyond wonder.

And as it points to the sky,
through it,
after being picked up by an angel,
engulfed in magic stardust,
soars at lightning speed, your loving mom,
as she leaves earth on her final journey.

And way, way, up there,
Where one can almost touch the stars,
forever sits, after a journey,
she could not quite finish.

Way, way up there, where infinite lies,
just look at the night sky,
and gaze at the shining star,
see how it glows,
watch how it sparkles.

That's her protecting you,
that's your mate and new journey companion,
now illuminating your road ahead,
as you complete your own journey through planet earth.

Way, way up there where one is in heaven,
where glittering rainbows end,
sits a new star,
that watches your back
and is your guardian forever.

"A Strong Group of Few"

Once upon a time,
There was this strong group of few,
They came from faraway lands,
They had Wills of Steel,
Their Flag was engraved on their Spirits,
Their Country was sculpted on their Souls,
And their loved ones carved on their Hearts.

And their Courage trumped any army,
obliterated any Fear,
and their overwhelming and indomitable Fury,
neither could be contained,
much less halted.

And when the time came to defend and conquer,
their Brave Hearts Roared,
and the Land Trembled,
and they fought for one another with Honor,
to defend and protect their Flag, Country, and Loved Ones.

Then the devastating force of their valor crushed it all,
leaving nothing in its wake.

Once upon a time,
There was this Strong Group of Few,
they came from faraway lands,
they had Brave Hearts
and they could not be conquered as
Their Flag was engraved on their Spirits,
Their Country was sculpted on their Souls,
And their loved ones carved on their Hearts.

"The Land of The Happy People"

Once upon a time,
in a land not so far from heaven,
there were quite a few Happy People,
but many more angry ones.

And, as they were more in numbers,
Happiness was usually overcome by Anger,
And this gave way to another awkward problem:
The majority was used to have their way,
hence, the happier the people got,
the angrier the others became.

Sometimes, it seemed like Happiness was not contagious enough.
Some others, it seemed like anger was the only thing that could be felt.

It all made up for an absurd and hard to define world,
as the angry people were uncomfortable, even resentful
with the permanent and unshakeable
sunny disposition and Happiness of the others.

Was it a Happy place dominated by Anger? or
Was it a place full of Anger dominated by Happiness?

Which did really have the power? Happiness or Anger?
Could an Angry person be Happy? Or even smile?
Was there any anger or pain in Happiness?
Could anger and Joy walk along side by side?
Could there be Joy when experiencing adversity and tragedy?

Did Angry people know how to be Happy?
Did Happy people know how to be Angry?
Did Angry people know what Happiness was?
Did Happy people know what Anger was?
Was there a formula on how to feel and be Happy?

Once upon a time,
in a land not so far from Heaven
there quite a few Happy people
that in the end prevailed over the many Angry ones
and ended Anger and Sadness forever.

"The Spinning Wheel of Life"

The spinning wheel of life goes around and around,
that's why everything we see,
comes and goes around in full circle
to the place where it started or where it ended.

Yes, in many ways life is a circle,
or better said,
a series of never-ending elliptical bends and curves,
of a bigger, wider circle.

And what seems new and unique to you,
has indeed already happened!
Millions of times before!

Because you see…
with each turn of the wheel,
what was,
what is,
and what will be,
are one of the same,
as in every one of life's turns,
there is a beginning,
then life takes us for a spin,
and then inevitably,
there is an end to everything.

But rejoice,
since the wheel endlessly spins,
each end is also a new beginning,
and as nothing stops,
life is, therefore,
a constant, circular, and flowing loop!
spinning and spinning,
around and around,

what is, is,
over and over,
what was,
will be,
what will be,
already was,
and will be again.

Let us treasure then,
as we circle around,
what already was,
and what is to come.

But above all,
let us rejoice in the here and now!
Especially those we love.
and for what we have, whatever that is,
as we don't really know,
when it will end.

But do not be distracted,
there are moments in one's life,
that start at the very end,
and others that end at the very beginning,
thus it is sound and astute to remember,
that an opening always awaits us in life,
the start of a new beginning.

Let us spin then
the wheel of life,
around and around,
we'll go in circles,
where the beginning,
the end,
and the middle of everything,
are one of the same,
just a different spin.

"Hope"

When things couldn't be worse or direr,
When all our strengths and fortitudes are gone,
Hope is what always pulls us through.

Hope is how we outlast adversity
and overcome every and any obstacle.
Hope is the life vest of our spirit and soul.

Hope is always our passport to freedom
from the shackles of our mind,
and the chains of hardship.

When there is hope,
we are not afraid of being afraid and there is simply,
no fear of fear itself.

Hope is always our safe-conduct
to the land of endurance and resilience.

Hope is always the seed of courage and valor,
Hope is one of the most powerful tools
to survive and make it through the "game of life."

Hope is that calming and steady inner power
that dotes us with bountiful confidence and steely resolve.

When there is hope we are always ready to restart,
rebuild, recreate, restore, renew, rekindle, repeat, rely, redo,
and remake it all, over and over and over again.

When we hope we are never willing to give up.
Hope in life and things, hope in oneself and others,
cures blindness and deafness in our soul and spirit,
filling life with shinning lights,
whispering tunes and melodies
on seemingly non-existing paths and non-existing doors.

Hope is our secret elixir for a life with purpose,
Hope is "the well of will" where we draw from,
to find meaning while we are alive.

While we hope,
we always stay true to ourselves and remain authentic.

Hope makes us feel invincible
against the most devastating weather systems,
Hope allows us to face the eye of any storm without blinking.

Hope equips us with stealth armor underneath soft gentle silk,
Hope enables us to always get back up and to never, ever, stay down.

We hope when we stubbornly believe we can make our future better,
and not only we know what we hope for,
but also, to a degree how we can do so.

Thus,
We hope when our determination
is more powerful than any circumstance
or anyone we may be facing
or any place in life's journey we may be at.

Hope feels great deep inside our core,
and that is why it is easily spread to others.

When we hope,
we deliberately chose to adopt a positive, resolute behavior.
That is why,
Hope is most enduring when along the way,
we knock out all our emotional roadblocks from its path.

Hope is far stronger when we hope
not only for our wellbeing, but also for others,
specially our loved ones.

When we hope, we stubbornly believe
there is always a solution
and a way in or out of everything.

When we hope against the tides
in spite of what oppresses and wounds us,
And when we hope with the belief
that the sacred and spiritual far transcend the mundane,
Then, hope becomes a shield
against failure, quitting or surrender,
an existential weapon
against pessimism or defeat.

Hope is a virtuous, elevated state of life
that exalts our human condition
and strengthens our character.

Hope's main virtue
is that makes us perennially resilient.

Hope's most powerful ammunition is courage and guts.

Hope is what builds and defines us as "life warriors"
ready to overcome and endure.

Hope is the ultimate exercise there is in self-determination,
and when there is no other left,
it is the last liberty standing,
enabling us to choose, pursue and battle,
regardless of anything or anyone,
to have a better future,
ahead of us.

"An Inspired Life"

To be inspired is to be continuously and blissfully happy,
to inhale deeply and feel really, really good inside
as we sigh in joy to the sweet taste
of purely and simply being alive.

Living an inspired life is a gift,
a magic incantation
that makes us life sorcerers,
of the kind that ask for nothing,
but dispense wizardry back in spades.

Behind an inspired person there's always that someone or something
that starts it all and that we connect so profoundly with.

Around an inspired person
there's always a powerful halo of positive energy,
a magnetic field that not only draws from our best talents,
but also attracts endless virtuous circles.

When we are inspired,
we are dressed in a mantle of immutability,
a permanent twinkle in our smile,
and eyes filled with the peace and calmness of a full life.

When we are inspired,
we contemplate life
through a magic magnifying glass as a rosy picture
even in the most trying of circumstances.
That is why, to be inspired requires
to be literally drenched in ingenuity and naivete.

When we are inspired,
all our best endowments are always on call,
ifs, buts, or cants are not in the picture
and there are no limits, boundaries, or periscopes
but wide and open horizons
for countless moonshots ahead of us.

For an inspired person
anything and everything is possible
as endless opportunities lie in waiting
to be tapped, discovered, and made.

It is a chance, an "unsculpted" rock,
an "uncrafted" melody, an unwritten verse,
an intimate and unpainted masterpiece yet to be born.

To live an inspired life is to be in a state of readiness
to capture the best life has to offer,
to squeeze the most out of our journey.

It is when life as a whole is fertile ground
for our dreams, fantasies, and imagination
and with all our good antennas up,
we acquire a noble altered state,
hypersensitive to anything worth pursuing.

When we are inspired,
there is no burden, drag or heaviness,
and everything becomes light, bright, and inviting.
Everything feels effortless.

Will moves mountains, inspiration while doing so, recreates them.

That's why inspiration renders will ordinary,
supersedes passion and conviction
and reduces self-confidence to a simple tool.

Sometimes inspiration hits us like a thunder bolt,
Some others it's simply a state,
a condition of sublime desire.

Sometimes to be inspired
is to be moved by Heaven and driven by Angels,
Some others it's to be provoked by the soul and sparked by the spirit,
but inspiration is always tuned and honed by our hearts.

When we are inspired,
we invent, create, tinker, build, craft, art, solve, visualize, foresee,
explain, understand, explore, seek, study, pray, love,
try and try and try, give back, do, make
and as a consequence, we live in full.

Inspiration is the stuff of wizards, life wizards that float through it all.

To be inspired,
to live an inspired life,
and to be an inspired person
is to be continuously and blissfully happy,
A kind of happiness
where we are permanently grateful to life,
A kind of happiness
where we continuously give and pay back,
A kind of "inspired happiness" that never goes away.

"The Past and The Future"

Conventional wisdom is such,
that when you do the wrong thing,
eventually the past catches up with you
and holds you accountable.

But there's also
the unspoken truth that,
when we fail to do in the present
what we are supposed to,
when we do not harness the power of now,
we are just postponing life itself,
and the future will eventually catch up with us, as well.

And we may not like it,
as it does not belong to us,
because we did not build or created it.
Bottom line, we won't own it.
It will own us.

So, we should ask ourselves,
are we postponing life?
do we keep pushing it forward?
the future is coming!
It is just around the corner
and when it finally arrives,
we may be stuck with it!

This until we start building our future
one day at a time now!
Then we will own it, and only then,
the future will be ours.

"Reach Out"

Lend a hand

Share a dream

Join in hope

Pray for others

Extend a favor

Give a kiss

Hug each other

Teach those in need

Learn from the wise

Take nothing

Always forgive

Use the strength of the truth

Love with passion

Remember your friends

Practice the power of humility

Shine on one another

Wait with grace and patience

Gift in earnest

Receive in Gratitude

Live with others

Give into someone's else's heart

Reach out, Reach out to Life!

"Winning is not for The Faint of Heart"

The road to victory is a game of survival.
It is war.
You visualize yourself as a gladiator in the arena,
a Stealth Ninja Warrior ready to attack in the shadows,
a Bullfighter charging into the fury of the beast.

You see yourself choosing between winning and losing
as if they were life or death.

You win when you want it so badly, it hurts inside,
You win when you want so much more than your opponent does.

You win when your mindset is that nothing,
except your values,
can stop you from achieving success.

You win when your sole purpose is to defeat your opponents.

You win by simultaneously
playing your strengths and your adversaries' weaknesses
or simply by flat-out outworking them!

You win when, deliberately and quietly
You try to capture each one
of your opponent's strengths and virtues.

You win when in your opponent's eyes,
You are fierce and steadfast
about your game plan and execution,
and yet, discreetly tweak and adapt it in a split second.

You win when, in preparation for a contest,
you approach every task with "tunnel vision"
and such steely resolve
that no one or nothing will prevent you from completing it.

Because "the art of winning" can only be mastered
by "paying every due" and "burning every candle"
as preparing to be ready to win is a long road
that has to be travelled in its entirety.

You win when you are one step ahead of your opponent
and still ask yourself, can I do it better?

You win when unflappable, you "keep on" going back again and again
to knock on the same door previously slammed in your face.

You win when a "no" is nothing but an invitation to try again.

You win when you are totally and utterly oblivious
to the word "rejection."

You win when you know when and how
to seek, take advice, and learn
from those who know how to win.

You win when you "take on" the better side of your ego
and make it your friend, your ally, and your weapon.

Because as opposed
to the shallowness and narcissism of arrogance,
self-confidence derives from knowledge and experience
and therefore is unshakable!

You win when through discipline and perseverance
you acquire the knowledge and experience
that will provide you the self-confidence
needed to master whatever you want to be the best at.

You win when you are willing and able to use
your anger as a source of strength,
when you morph your rage into a burning and unstoppable desire,
and when you draw from your "well of will"
the fire and the fury needed to win.

You only win after you've experienced
countless losses, defeats, stumbles, and fumbles,
and the worse they have been,
the better prepared you are to win in the future.

But for a path to victory
one has to harness one's very own demons,
one has to "rein in" a unique cast of "free spirited" characters
that inhabit the kingdoms of our mind and spirit.

That's why in order to win
we have to conquer our own mountains,
break down walls,
vanquish enemy armies,
annihilate pessimists,
ridicule the skeptical,
render mute the excusers and naysayers,
exile the slouches,
calm the fearful, making them our allies,
and turn the doubters into charlatans,
and we have to do it all within the confines of ourselves,
as we do it, when in battle.

Sometimes winning requires you to follow your gut,
your better fibers, your most animalistic, atavistic, and primal instincts,
all shaken and stirred into a cocktail of "raw passion."

Sometimes winning requires you to follow your brain,
your rational thinking, your battle plans, strategy, and logic.

Often you require both!
Even though on any given Sunday,
in the game of winning, passion generally beats brains!

You win when you enjoy and share
the spoils from the act of winning,
You win when you live, appreciate and value,
the journey to victory,
You win when it brings out the best in you,
You win when it makes you better,
When you win you celebrate life.

But above all,
You win when you are not fooled by it.
On the contrary, keep it in its right place,
as winning even though an essential component of life,
is only a "Game of Life."

It is not existential or sacred but mundane and passing,
It is not love or friendship,
neither truth nor faith,
and it is not virtue or values,
but only a "will and grit" booster, a worthy test of the intensity
with which you live your life.

Winning is not for the faint of heart
as it requires boundless courage and strength.

Winning is for those
that challenge and defy life with their hearts
and for who living a life in full,
inexorably includes the tenacity of winning
as an "intrinsical" part of the equation,
to squeeze out of life
the sublime passion of victory.

"Self-Reliance"

Self-Reliance is the action and life of self-assertiveness.
It is to be accountable first and foremost to oneself.
Is the realization that I am able to rely on myself
before anyone or anything,
and but for reasons,
of love, generosity, a moral imperative,
or a combination of any of them,
I can put others before or ahead of me in the endeavors of my life.
When it comes to dependence though,
I depend on no one, but myself.

I depend on myself first before I depend on others
as I shall never expect, count, or rely
on others to act on my behalf or even do for me,
What I am supposed to do,
What only I can do,
What only I should do,
by myself.

Also, I rely on myself and what I believe in,
irrespective and above what others believe.

As I rely on myself first,
I am immune to the opinions and influence of others.
I rely on myself despite what society thinks.

I rely on my instincts and my gut,
not instead,
but before any norm, rule, or law.

As I rely on myself,
I break away, inoculate against,
or do not fall into the chains of conformism, indoctrination,
or the annihilation and disappearance of myself.

I rely on myself first as it is the only way
I can establish my individuality, my character, my personality,
in other words, my identity.

I rely on myself first
because is the foundation of my independence
and the seed of my sense
of self-worth, self-respect, and dignity.

If I can govern myself without the belief,
without the help or influence of anyone,
then I have acquired all of the above.

I am able to rely on myself first if I think, feel and act
with integrity, without impulsiveness
and according to
my spiritual, moral-ethical, and family values.

I rely on myself first because I trust myself,
and, as result, believe in and have self-confidence
to face life as myself and not as someone else,
with all my capacities, talents,
always true to my identity.

"The Better Instincts of Our Hearts"

There are things in life
that we can only do from our hearts,
and those we never regret.

In fact, we'll do them over and over again the same exact way.

These are acts of life
where we draw from the better instincts of our hearts,
and as they are driven mainly
by passion, convictions, and principles.
Self-interest or consequences don't matter,
as much as one's self-beliefs,
for that someone, whom,
we are ready to take a bullet for.

One thing is absolutely certain,
these types of monumental steps are not driven by our brains!
Because we could never have the courage and unselfishness
to hurt ourselves or act against our own best interests,
as both are exclusively matters of the heart.

These acts of valor are where heroes are born,
the course of history is changed,
lives are spared or saved,
and humanity shines and rises to its highest levels.

There are many of us
who are born with great instincts of the mind,
and there are also many of us
who come to life with great instincts of the heart,
but one of life's paradoxes is
that we always seem to follow
those instincts that we are the weakest on,
inevitably leading us
into unfulfilled and depressing lives.

And in matters of love,
the brain and the heart are like oil and water,

they don't mix well,
because the brain
cannot create, govern, control, or sustain love
nor vice-versa.

When we follow
the better instincts of our brains in matters of love,
there is no love,
but rather thoughts instead of feelings.

What likely there is,
is an arrangement where we settle for comfort and emptiness.

Because inasmuch as
the better instincts of our minds serve us well,
when logic, convenience and common sense are required,
when looking back at life,
we will always realize
that immense, absolute, and wholesome happiness
only comes to us
when we've followed
the better instincts of our hearts.

"Life Is Bliss"
(The Importance of The Small Details in life)

If you want to live a blissful life,
pay attention to "the little details"
both on the receiving and giving ends of it.

But not the kind where "the devil is in the…"
as those are easy and hidden in plain sight,
and they are usually expected rules, norms, or stipulations,
we either follow, ignore, break, or circumvent.

So, they are narrow in human nature and binary in their scope,
as they simply bite you or they don't.

No, to live a life in bliss you have to pay attention
to a different kind of little details,
those that are gestures of love,
those that come straight from the heart.

They are usually spontaneous and unexpected,
often hold very little or no material value,
but always provide immense bliss and joy,
the kind when it is hard to breathe
in the throats of both the dispenser and the recipient
as emotions bundle up in a knot.

These types of little details require genial creativity,
but that becomes easy when propelled
by overwhelming empathy and caring for others.

When we receive these little details,
they hold their biggest value,
when we are richer, in health
and things are better, well and good,
yet we are still humble enough
to pay attention, to appreciate and value
how much we are loved by others.

When we give, the little details have their greatest worth,
when we are poorer, in sickness,
things are at their worst, not good or simply bad,
and we still have the heart and the desire
to give to others for whom we care about.

It is on those extremes,
valuing what we are offered when we don't need it,
or caring about giving the little we have left,
when small details in life matter the most,
become unforgettable, never leave,
and stay with us forever.

Life is bliss when caught by surprise, overcome by emotion
we hide our face behind the palms of our hands,
or when we find that loving note in our pocket
or leave that flower on her pillow,
or in those tiny precious gestures
that mom, dad, granny, and grandpa never forget.

Those little things that never fail to be there,
that supportive hug or kiss,
that reassuring or uplifting smile,
that contagious laughter,
those calming, maybe loving, perhaps tender and grateful eyes,
any or all of these little things that make us react in bliss:
What a gesture, they love me,
oh my, I love her, him, them, you with all my heart.

So, if you want to live life in bliss,
pay close attention to the small details in life,
those that come straight from the heart,
those that are spontaneous gestures of love,
those that are just little things,
those that we offer and receive with absolute joy,
those that we never forget for the rest of our lives.

"Love's Rabbit Hole"

How do you know when love is knocking at your door?
How do you know when it is arrived?
And its music, the music of angels,
is all out there waiting for you.

How do you know that whoever's reached you
is maybe that travel mate
you've been wishing for all along?

And how do you know its time,
right there and then to come out of your shell
and knock down your protective shields.

You know it,
because when that someone
unexpectedly irrupts into your life's journey
it simply takes your breath away.

You know it, because,
when you can finally catch your breath,
all you inhale, feels like at that moment,
there is absolutely nothing else you would like to be doing
nor is there anyone else in the world
you would like to be with, than your rabbit.

You know it, because,
the world around you disappears
and you willingly fall through
the most "scintillatious" rabbit hole
you'll ever find in your life.

You know it when out of the blue,
the object of your desire can't do or say anything wrong,
as all you see is perfection
through benevolent magnifying glasses
made out of boundless candor, ingenuity, and romance.

You know it, when from the get-go,
you feel comfortable, confident, and light on your feet
and life becomes a journey of two,
impregnated with magic, happiness, passion, and joy.

You know it, because,
you become possessed with this inexplicable certainty
that you are safe, protected and never alone.

And You know it when you see yourself
visualizing your life, your future, your family, and your children,
only through and with your other half.

And you know it, because Love's Rabbit Hole is one
From which you'll never want to get out from.

"The Secret Lies in Opposite Ends At Work Forever"

You like to dance, and I don't.

You are spontaneous and blunt, and I am not.

You are loud and noisy; I am silence personified.

You are social and friendly; I am not very much of either.

You have a short fuse that erupts and fades like a volcano;
my flame burns slowly for a long time.

You like to sleep late; I rise early way before dawn.

You plan way ahead; I do everything at the last minute.

You love to constantly organize everything around you;
I like everything organized most of the time.

You make cleanliness and neatness happen at all times;
I enjoy them both immensely.

You can remember certain things well;
I always remember others quite well too.

You read many people with absolute accuracy;
I always read others, but not all that well as you do.

You love a good wine and cheese;
I am still learning to do the same.

You are a great and lightning-fast cook;
I have no idea how to cook at all.

You don't care much for breakfast,
for me it's the most important meal of the day.

You don't like ice-cream or chocolates,
I love them both to no end.

You are effusive in celebration,
I am hardly expressive on those occasions.

You play instruments with ease,
I have no clue how to do that either.

You love certain kinds of music with passion;
I love all kinds of music from all over the world.

You aren't grabby or touchy-feely,
I am all of that, all of the time.

You can be ferociously jealous at times,
for me those are just games people play.

You call everything by its name;
I use terms of endearment for everyone and everything.

You like routines and predictability,
I am exactly the opposite to that.

You don't l like being naked, less being barefoot,
I am quite the contrary on those as well.

You like to talk non-stop about anything,
I only do when I am passionate about something.

You like me to read to you, I do that with gusto.

You never understand any movie,
but always stay awake throughout,
I always fall asleep on them
but somehow still manage to explain them to you afterwards!

You always fall asleep when I drive,
I take us both to our destination,
talking to myself the whole trip.

You hate to be behind the wheel; I can drive forever.

You can become grumpy when bored,
those words do not exist in my vocabulary.

You never like what you order at a restaurant;
I always feed you, otherwise you help yourself to what I've ordered.

You are cautious and fearful,
I don't understand any of those words either.

You are full of laughter,
mine are hard to come by.

You love a good dress and wear it well;
I never pay any attention to mine.

We couldn't be more different about with
Whom, How, When, Where, and What we work at,
And yet, we couldn't be more alike in how hard we go at it!

You type superfast, I hardly do it at all.

Yet, I read superfast, and you don't.

You hate to carry anything,
It has never bothered me to do it for you.

You never know where you are; I am like a human compass.

You never know how to get there;
Most of the time I don't need a map.

You don't know how to strike a bargain, or negotiate a price,
I love to do both.

You believe many things are impossible;
I believe almost anything is possible,
and you've trusted me with that.

You like to sit down, be waitered on, and enjoy a good meal;
I prefer self-service.

You like a good, loud fight;
I am Mr. quiet, anti-noise, and anti-fight.

You don't overlook anything you dislike;
I consciously distort reality.

You stumble and fumble all the time,
I'm not much better at that at all.

You love to browse and hardly ever shop,
I can't wait to get out.

You are very hard to please when you want something.
I am always dead-on, on size, type, and style when I do it for you.

Your fears go away on board and card games,
where you cheat all the time.
while I am naive, clumsy, foolish,
and an easy prey for you on them.

Your fears also go out of the window when it comes to jumping lines,
I am always embarrassed and hesitant, but obediently follow your lead.

You are a terrible cyclist, I am a terrific one.

You are a great swimmer,
for me, mediocre would be a superlative when doing that.

You like the beach without sand on your feet;
I was raised on the beach and love as it is, wild and dirty.

You like perfectly tranquil and glorious weather,
the tougher and rougher it is, the better for me.

I am overwhelmingly physical,
You are always successful in slowing me down.

You are claustrophobic;
I have motion sickness.

You are afraid of heights;
I prefer rooms with a view from floor to ceiling.

You don't mind sitting in the middle;
I always sit in the front, the aisle or facing the crowd.

You love ballet and the opera;
I love a good philharmonic orchestra, and a good library.

We both love museums, just different parts of them.

You like to sit and munch;
I can spend hours at a bookstore or looking at historical pictures.

You curse and use loaded words,
I never do so.

For you it's very hard to move on or let go,
for me it's just a flick of a switch away.

You love to run but no longer can;
for me running is a way of life.

The things we agree on,
are easy to spot and write endlessly about.

But it is on the things we are not alike,
where healthy tension abounds.

That's why the secret lies on two opposite ends
working together forever.

"What Is Love?"

What a bewildering feat,
a pair of souls, smitten for one another,
the whispering and whistling of a pair of infatuated hearts,
in a world all of their own.

The peace and ease of two spirits
totally comfortable with each other, at all times,
while enjoying the most sublime of connections,
in a place where innate beauty lies in bunches.

A twosome in a state of constant flux,
where everything begins and then continues
through endless reactions
to one another's expressions of love.

And by wrapping themselves around each other's fingers,
they literally surrender to one another,
and seemingly do with each other, what they please.

And then forever spoiled,
neither is ever able to accept anything less,
but exactly the same or more,
from their other half.

That is how love becomes a perennial exercise
of placing themselves in each other's shoes,
that is why love is the ultimate empathy of two hearts
possessed by each another
always and forever.

"What Is True Love?"

True Love is,
When your heart does not belong to you.

True Love is,
When your life's glass is only full when with your loved one.

True Love is,
When you feel you can move mountains
or split oceans for one another.

True Love hears and sees no evil,
as it is unconditional, no matter the deed or mischief.

True Love is,
When your skin aches
without your other half's touch
and nothing is warmer
than being in each other's arms.

True Love is,
When passion is so overwhelming
that it's just one flick of a switch away.

True Love is,
When success, defeat or failure don't matter,
when pain and joy neither.

It is to be all for each other,
it is when we give everything, and then some.

True Love is also on the greetings
that make us jump up and down,
and the long embraces and farewells
that leave us unable to swallow or breath.

True Love is,
When we patiently wait and hope
without really expecting anything in return.
True love is also,
in the benign and forgiving stare,
and in the smiles bursting with joy,
and in the laughter's
which are our life's "echoes of happiness."

True Love is,
When your soul mate
is part of your very essence.
When your spirit is split between the two of you,
and both souls have surrendered fusing into one,
while becoming travel mates
in the topsy-turvy journey of life.

True Love is,
When the colors of life, shine and blossom in full,
the Bells of Heaven ring,
and life's orchestra plays as its best,
and everything we feel is as if we were at Ecstasy's Zenith.

True Love can't be measured,
True Love can't be controlled,
True Love is empowering,
True Love is one of Life's greatest gifts,
it is precious, and many times overlooked.

True Love is hard to find most likely you never will.
It will find you!

True Love is a miracle,
and one of the great wonders of being alive.

"The Three-Legged Stool"

What makes a great couple?

First comes Friendship,
Its foundations are
Honesty, Loyalty, Fidelity, and Commitment.
In them reside communication and the sharing of everything.

It is trusting to no end.

It is giving without expecting anything in return.
It is knowing what the other thinks without words,
and sensing what the other wants with just a glance.

It is completing each other sentences,
complementing each other's weaknesses and differences.
It is where respect and admiration are the drivers and support columns.

It is where true intimacy lies,
and where the walls and boundaries of a twosome
are built like a fortress that provides haven
for comfort, safety, privacy, and strength to one another.

When there is true intimacy,
our other half becomes the person
whom we are comfortable with at all times,
whom we never tire to see, talk, or share with.

It is the person that sometimes is our parent,
some others a sibling, many others a spouse or simply a friend.

It is the person that motivates us the most,
but also, calls us out, and makes us stop,
change course or make amends.

True friendship thrives on a healthy level of tension,
and it is where,
for better or worse, in sickness or in health, and for richer or poorer, lie.

Second comes Passion,
That's when the flesh explodes without control,
when blood and desire are like a fireball,
two bodies are insatiable,
and cannot get enough of each other,
no matter how, no matter when, no matter where.

It is when lust overwhelms and takes-over mind and body,
it is when one look, one touch,
one movement, one thought, one image
is all it takes for arousal to go galore! Both ways,

It is when fantasy and imagination become reality in a "flash of flesh."
It is when everything about the other is
sensual, carnal, and seductive
all the time and at any time.

Third, comes Love,
True Love is when your heart does not belong to you.
True Love is when the bells of Heaven are ringing,
and the Trumpets of Life
play heart-shaped musical notes at full throttle.

It is the delicate rose garden
that requires constant, tender care,
producing immense, but tender and fragile beauty.

True love is when your skin aches missing your other half's touch.

It is to be endlessly in awe, hopelessly infatuated,
and carelessly wrapped around each other's fingers,
and when nothing is warmer than being in each other's arms.
True Love is gallantry and courtship,
It is poetry and total surrender.

It is when the colors of life shine and blossom in full
and life's orchestra plays at its best,
and everything we feel is as if
we were at "Ecstasy's Pinnacle."

Friendship, Passion, and Love
are the three legs of a stool
that depict a wholesome couple,
a couple that will last and endure life,
a couple that will stay together forever.

"Sorting out The Rest"

Of all the "ifs" and "buts" we face none are more powerful
that the ones coming from those who provide us
with living tutelage and life lessons.

At first, we may pretend we don't listen to them,
we in fact, may not even do so at first.

But somewhere, somehow along the
way, hopefully sooner more often than
later,
those words of wisdom almost always,
finally register.
And as we sort everything else out,
it is what was wisely said once,
what may come to us at the right time,
hopefully guiding,
maybe even preventing,
or even if after the fact,
helping us know what to do,
perhaps even how to mend,
the next time around.

"If I could Find You Out There"

If I could touch the stars with my heart,
the night darkness would turn into
reds of roses and reds of fire.

If I could reach the sky with my dreams,
the colors and tones of daylight would turn into
inspired whites and passionate blues.

If I could morph into words,
those life moments that touch the soul, they would turn into
endless hues and shades of wisdom.

If I could simply be art, of the kind that brings joy to the spirit,
it would turn into greens of plenitude and yellows of life.

If I could fly to the moon and gaze back at our planet earth,
it would glow like a magnificent rainbow turning into
every color there could ever be.

But if I could only find you,
somewhere, out there in the Universe,
my dreams and my passions,
my spirit and my soul,
my life and my heart,
and the totality of my world,
they would all,
turn into you.

If I could only find you out there, somewhere in the Universe.

"A Labor of Love"

What a tough job to have to navigate
through the darkest corners
of the minds of others,
rather than your own.

Those paths where the ground is shaky,
where the foundations have cracks,
where the earth moves,
where some of the tracks of life are blurry,
without enough light,
and there is no sense of wellbeing or happiness.

But perhaps there is no tougher job than
that of dealing with minds
that not only lack such meaning and purpose in life,
but are also potentially or inherently
wicked, devious, reckless, delusional,
or simply love themselves so much
that there is no room or care for anyone else.

Hence, it is only because of this awesome labor
of deeply rooted vocational love for the wellbeing of others,
that such worthy endeavor
makes that big a difference in the lives of many.

The type of non-stop steady effort
that addresses every obstacle and every crisis
or extreme situation with resolve and genial creativity,
the kind that connects with each individual
and makes them feel and believe
not only that they are unique, respected, and worthy,
but above all,
also "Able to" grow, overcome, and have a future,
as long as they are willing to shape-up, do the work,
and perform at high standards.

What a tough job doing good,
by improving the mindset of others in need,
what an impossible job to perform
for those in need of redemption,
those in need of a second act in life,
those that very few support or believe in.

What a tough job,
What an impossible job,
What an impactful task,
What a wonderful labor of love,
that's what you'll do,
that's what you will be leaving in your wake,
that's what you would have done!

"There Is a Life To Be Lived Out There"

Is there anything, anything?
that we seek, but never reach?

Is there someone, yes, that someone
that we wait for, but never find?

Is there someone, anyone that we don't need,
but never leaves?

Is there a place, yes, that place that we miss,
but never seek?

Is there a moment that we want back,
but is already gone forever?

Is there something, yes, something that we lost,
but never search for?

Are there many, yes, many things that we have to learn,
but never do?

Are there a few words, yes, those words
that we could or should have said
but never did?

Is there such a person
that brings us joy and happiness,
but we don't appreciate it?

Is there a moment in time that we regret
but it's too late?

Is there such a friend or loved one that gives us so
much, without asking anything in return,
but we don't value enough?

Is there a time, a moment, a place
where we must stop or pause,
but we don't?

Is there a secret, yes, that secret
that we must have known or perhaps shared,
but never did?

Is there a past, yes, that past
that eventually will catch up with us, but
we never made amends to prevent it?

Is there a wait, a long wait that we endured to no avail,
but quit when it reoccurred again?

Are there family and friends, yes, family and friends
to be loved and cherished,
but we fall short?

Is there that little, tiny, teeny detail that we should have given
but didn't?

Is there that true love, yes, that love waiting for us,
that we never go for it?

Is there a God to fear, believe and get close to
but we fail to do so?

Is there happiness
to be found and enjoyed everywhere but we don't seem to find it?

Is there inspiration
in many little, simple but important, and essential things
yet, we aren't able to notice them?

Is there compassion to gracefully give to others,
but we can't feel it?

Is there forgiveness to be dispensed
but we can't get to act on it?

Is there hope
for a better life and circumstances,
but we abandon it?

Is there so much to be provided for,
but we fail to do so?

Is there a lot needed by others, yes, needed by others,
but we fail to recognize it?

Is there a future not to be postponed,
is there a world, our world,
to be seized, to be squeezed, to be lived,
just with spirit and desire?

Is there a life
without "ifs" or "buts"
without negative, regretful, or lingering grudges?

A world to give, receive and enjoy.
A life, our life,
the only one we've got,
the only one we will ever have.

Yes, there is!
There is a life, and a world ready to be lived,
waiting for all of us,
and it's happening right now.

"Life's True Success Is Being Happy"
(Life is Not A Spectator Sport)

Life is not a spectator's sport,
if you want to be entertained, you will,
as life will offer you countless options
to choose from a never-ending carrousel.

But once the show is over,
the fun and the thrill of it all will escape you in a hurry,
as being a spectator makes it impossible to capture and retain
the passion and the purpose of what others did.

Feeling good for long never happens to the bystander,
as the emptiness of a life without meaning
will sink and settle in
when you are alone at night with your own pillow.

You can yell, scream, celebrate and rejoice
in the victories and defeats of others all you want,
but it'll be only for a fleeting moment,
because in the end, you are still you,
and nothing's changed.

Life, to the contrary,
is a participant's sport
where you play with passion and purpose
which in turn brings you happiness and meaning,
and those two last only as long as
you continue to churn and churn
pouring your heart out into everything that you do.

A life with passion and purpose
is one where you are its main participant.
It's a life where you rise and fall, you win and lose,
you love, and in return and loved back,
and where you give out a lot more that you receive or take in.
It's a life where you dare, endure and stumble,
but never stop trying or give up!

It's a life where you are endlessly curious and always learning.
It's a life in which you are totally immerse and involved.
It's a life with a meaning, it's a life in full.

It is a life where happiness is not pursued
but ensues as a result of your deliberate involvement
in a wholesome living experience.

Because in the end,
what you really want is <u>existential success,</u>
what you are really after is <u>vital achievement</u>.

But there's no success or achievement of any kind as a spectator,
only fun and intensity
that are both shallow and passing.

Success or achievement do not belong to the spectators or bystanders,
they belong to life's players,
those that are involved,
"<u>The Participants</u>."

Life's truest success is being happy,
as happiness is perhaps the highest level of existential success,
one where you can never cease to be totally involved in,
one that once you create a virtuous circle,
it never ends.

"The Happiness Formula"

Sometimes, we hope, that simply by being alive,
happiness will be something
we will find or stumble onto
with utmost certainty.

But waiting for happiness to occur by chance or luck
is the equivalent of a reward without merits
or a price gained
without struggle or effort.

In other instances, we wish,
that happiness would be cast on us through a "magic spell,"
an incantation, a dream, or an illusion.

But there aren't too many existential sorcerers among us,
as life wizards are very hard to find,
since the formula to morph dreams into happiness
is an exceptional virtue that very few possess.

Why is happiness so elusive, unexpected, and ephemeral?
Can we ever find it?
and if we do,
Would we recognize it?
Would we know it?
If so,
Would we enjoy it?
Would we be appreciative of the privilege?
And then treasure it afterwards?
Some believe that in order to attain happiness it must be pursued.
Hence, it is a derivation from a deliberate chase
or pursuit that makes it happen.

There are others who to the contrary, believe that happiness ensues,
as a "consequence of" or is "subsequent to" and therefore
is the outcome of the pertinent ways we choose to live our lives.

Then, there are those who believe that happiness
only occurs in the face of tragedy and sorrow.
But tragic optimism, pain and suffering are rarely a path to Joy!

So, how do we find happiness?
Do we find it through the intention and desire to be happy?
Or do we find it through the paths and roads
we willfully take towards the land of joy?
Or through both?

The answer lies in The Happiness Formula, which is defined,
by three interconnected life attitudes and three supporting blocks:

First,
Find your Passion.
Passion is your life's engine.
Seek and discover what your love. Engage and do it!

Recognize your passions, pursue, and stick to them
as this will greatly enhance the chances,
that your strongest talents and abilities
will emerge and be put to good use,
causing you to perform
at whatever endeavor you chose,
to the fullest of your abilities.

To do what you love is easy,
and the energy, determination, discipline, and persistence required
feel effortless, inviting, and without obstacles.

When you do what you love,
it brings you the greatest amount
of satisfaction, pride, and sense of accomplishment.

When you do what you are passionate about,
you will never find "ifs" "buts" or "excuses"
hindering you to get started,
nor will you talk yourself into inaction
or avoid your duties and obligations.

But to be a master of anything
takes time, growth, maturity, determination,
failure, innate talent, and passion.

Second,
Productivity requires Tempo.
Tempo is your life's engines RPMs.
It is the pace at which you execute and deliver.

It is about how efficient you are.
Without rhythm and tempo, you are quickly overwhelmed
and your productivity, effectiveness, efficiency
and life's engine, slow down.

In today's world an engine without the right RPMs,
overheat and overloads in a heartbeat.

Besides, in order to multitask and cope
with the pace of modern life,
in order to be "highly functional,"
and in order to be able to sustain a high Tempo,
you will need to constantly re-train and re-calibrate yourself,
so, you can perform at a Tempo
commensurate with your lifestyle and goals.

And Third,
Being alive requires Awareness.
Capture and expand your life
through "deliberate vital engagement."
We cannot be bystanders of our own lives.
We must be active participants,
totally involved in our existence,
capturing each of its moments,
exactly as they are dealt to us.

We can't postpone our lives,
We can't afford to allow our precious time on planet earth,
be simply about day after day, rolling on top of each other
while we are bystanders observing from afar
in a catatonic, zombie-like state.

We must be eternally grateful as well,
for what we and our travel mates in life
have and receive every day.

Passivity is out of the question. Action is an existential imperative!

Finally, life gives us minute signs,
teeny-tiny, but crucial important messages containing clues
that without awareness,
we may not be able to see,
as if we were walking blindly through it.

One thing is absolutely certain,
sometimes as symbols of life,
these light bulbs will be scattered,
and sprinkled along our journey's path.

Some others as calls to action or simply as warning signs,
but all of them waiting for us
to be spotted and figured out
as if they were puzzles that once solved
will light up our way,
enabling us to move forward in life,
with a fully lit road ahead of us.

But three supporting blocks are needed for happiness to thrive:

First,
You need Love to be happy.
Love is the foundation of happiness,
True Love is when your heart does not belong to you.
Focus on giving out of your heart and do it with passion.

Second,
You need Balance (equilibrium) between fun and work.
Set and keep your priorities in balance.

Balance only exists
when there's a solid emotional life underneath, supporting us.

Equilibrium is born
out of trial and error, endless practice, and a healthy lifestyle.

And Third,
Happiness thrives on solid Values.
Character and Virtue are built out of
Spiritual, Moral and Family values
through faith, truth, honesty,
and unbreakable bonds of love.

Out of this happiness ecosystem of three attitudes
(*Passion, Tempo, and Awareness*)
and three foundations supporting them
(*Love, Balance, and Values*)
is where inspiration born, where inspiration thrives,
propelling us into a noble condition of sublime desire
as well as a highly functional state
that brings out the best in all of us,
generating continuous happiness.

Inspiration may well be
the only source of continuous happiness.
Inspiration is the stuff of wizards.
Life Wizards!

"The Happiness Triangle"

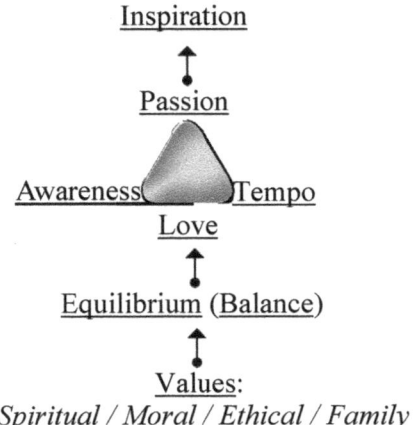

"Optimism"

Optimism is a deliberate attitude
where we chose to contemplate life and its people,
through their best lights, colors, and mantels.

It is a predisposition to look, search and find,
the better angle and perspective,
on everything and everyone.

It is a natural inclination to visualize,
what is the best,
a person or a circumstance has to offer.

It is that refreshing enthusiasm
we bring into all and every one of life's occurrences,
any and each of its moments.

It is that unquenchable certainty, that there always is,
a shinier side and a brighter spot to be found.

It is that steadfast and indomitable self-confidence,
that there's always
a better outcome possible,
in store waiting for us.

Optimism also is,
that gentle, benign, immutable self-belief
that there is goodness on the other side of evil,
strength in the other face of weakness,
virtue behind every flaw,
opportunity when apparently there is none,
incandescence in obscurity,
and luminescence in darkness.

Those possessed with optimism
live in another world, live an alternate life, and contemplate it all
with a permanent twinkle in their eyes.

Optimists are always
cheerful, self-motivated, fiercely determined,
and seemingly possessed with a secret elixir
that allows them to erase and wipe out,
pessimism, prejudice, negativism, and grudges,
from their lives.

Optimism always obliterates,
"The loser before the start" syndrome, from all of us.

With optimism we see past or right through everything and everyone.

Civilization has been built out of optimism,
progress is driven by optimism,
every single human invention, creation, or advancement,
has taken place through
the candor, the innocence, and the ingenuity of optimists.

And not a single transcendental milestone in humanity,
will ever be reached, done, or achieved,
without the unstoppable drive of optimism.

True, legitimate a genuine optimism always marches forward
cannot be deterred, deviated, or turned back.

Optimism is utterly oblivious
to criticism, rejection, doubt, or skepticism.

Authentic optimism is also malleable,
that is why, the tougher the goals, obstacles or challenges,
the bigger genuine optimism becomes.

Those bitten by the bug of optimism,
have "good blinders on"
making them immune to the contrarians and nay Sayers.

In their own way
optimists intentionally "distort reality,"
until the alternate version of it, becomes the new reality.

Then, they enhance whatever there is available to them,
through a perennially benevolent and candid vision, of
what, may, could, would, might and inexorably,
under such a state and condition,
will be.

"Small Sacrifices"

Sometimes life presents us
with seemingly impossible tasks,
and insurmountable challenges,
so demanding,
that we don't really know where to begin,
much less if we can respond or live up to them,
or even if we will be able
to hold on to the very end.

Sometimes life presents us with seemingly huge sacrifices,
that more often than not,
come dressed in tragedy and pain.

Those moments test our entire self,
and every task expected of us,
is tough, trying, unsavory, and even filthy,
to execute and endure.

These calls of duty present themselves to us
as very difficult sacrifices,
ones where every inch and instinct
of our ego and selfishness,
reject and easily finds excuses
to avoid, even start, anything at all.

They may include the people close to us,
that cannot take care of themselves
or are handicapped, even terminally ill,
need assistance day in and day out,
and for a while, for long
or for the remainder of their lives,
they are entirely in our hands.

Then there are those,
that are deprived of their freedom,
depending on, or relying
on our love, strength, and support
as we depend on theirs.

There are also,
those that are hungry or homeless,
or those in need of guidance, mentoring,
tutoring, coaching, or life lessons,
and yet none have anything to offer us,
in the way of material things.

These are some of those moments,
when Life and God,
come calling to test us on
How good we are deep inside?

What is our quality and worthiness as human beings?
What is our heart really made of?
How ready are we to sacrifice and give much
without truly expecting anything in return.

In reality,
these are just small sacrifices and in a way gifts,
that are asked and required of us
in return for all of those
that we receive and have received in the past.

Sometimes life presents us with seemingly huge sacrifices,
that are not such,
as they are opportunities for us to pay forward,
the greatest gift of all,
one already given to us in kind,
"The Gift of Life."

"Of Fate and Fairy Tales"

Where does a fairy tale begin? How does it start?
How is it created? Where can we find one?
And once we do, how do we turn it on?
When is it that our life's pages,
shine and sparkle in of all their splendor,
and our hearts are suddenly filled
with magical dreams and reciprocal love?

It is commonly said and acknowledged that fate is:
predictable, unavoidable, ineludible, inescapable, inevitable,
making us mere terrestrial beings
careening through the existential universe,
towards pre-planned destinations or outcomes.

Such a belief is not only false,
it is also crucially wrong
as it derails our spirits under the conviction
that our lives occur in some sort of pre-ordained fashion.

But fate is just a banal excuse,
dressed under a fake historical costume of legitimacy.
Its only purpose is to justify a non-deliberate life,
one that lacks meaning and purpose.

Fact is, we create our own fairy tales,
it is on us, no one else.

We can make a fairy tale out of anything, anyone or anywhere.
Life is a never-ending fairy tale if we make it such.

There is extraordinaire, magnificence,
"splendorness," felicitousness and awesomeness,
around every corner, right in front of us,
as well as inside each one of us,
ready to be uncovered and released,
as long as we are able to see life and its people
with a touch of candor, ingenuity, and good faith.

And yet, there is nothing accidental or fortuitous about fairy tales.

> Many of us think that someday we are going to run
> into a fairy godmother, a wizard, or an enchantress,
> or even a prince on a white horse,
> or a goddess of virtue, beauty, and strength,
> that will sweep us off our feet.
>
> What we have to realize though,
> is that we are each one of those characters already,
> as they all reside within our own spirits.
>
> So, how do we turn a fairy tale on?
> First and foremost, by leaving nothing to chance!
> And with an unquenchable desire to live, love and dream.
>
> Also, by recognizing, appreciating, and pursuing
> the inner beauty that resides in each human being,
> no matter who they are.
>
> And by understanding that,
> no matter how dire life may be,
> every circumstance, every moment,
> every challenge, obstacle, or hardship,
> no matter how unsavory they may seem,
> every failure, defeat, or rejection,
> no matter how deflating, they may appear,
> they all have not only existential value,
> but also enchantment,
> for us to discover, enjoy, and experience.

"My Radiant Goddess of The Night"

Here we are
under a star-studded sky,
in the silence of the night,
over the moist
but still warm sands
of an empty beach.

Here we are on this magic island
where our story,
the one that is only about the two of us,
has begun.

My Radiant Goddess of The Night.
Where are you taking me?
Where are you taking us?
With this nascent love.

When I see you, I sigh in joy,
just with your presence.

When you look at me
my infatuated heart,
makes me tremble.

Just one touch or slight brush
from that warm silky skin of yours
makes me moan all over in ecstasy filled desire.

And when you embrace me
I feel this inexplicable plenitude, a blissful certitude,
that I am at a safe harbor, protected and no longer alone.

My Radiant Goddess of The Night,
Where are you taking us?
Where are you taking me?
With this nascent love of mine.

"There Is Something About You"

Ever since that day we met,
there is something about you,
that makes life magical.

Don't ask me how,
but it is this irresistible
and wickedly beautiful spell you cast,
that simply makes us happy, whole, and safe.

There is something about you,
that colors everything,
and makes of every sunrise a wonderful beginning,
every sunset, not only a glorious end,
but also, a continuous spin with a new beginning.

There is something about you,
that always feels cozily anew.

There is something very special about you,
that makes love come alive,
and one twinkles, shivers and breaths deep
while wearing a never-ending smile.

There is something about you,
that enraptures my heart,
and makes it forever yours.

"Life, Character and Virtue"

One's character is our calling card to life,
as well as,
the legacy our wake leaves behind.

Our character defines not who we think we are,
much less what we pretend to be,
but who we really are, deep, deep, inside.

Our character is respected when,
we exude immutable honesty and steadfast frankness.

Our character is emulated when,
we are uncompromisingly ethical,
approach everything
with unquestionable rectitude, indomitable integrity,
while beholding,
a spirit with a purpose and a soul with meaning.

Our character is revered when in possession of
limitless compassion, unmaterialistic generosity,
and the humblest of all wisdoms.

Our character becomes reliable through,
dependable, and immanent self-discipline.

Our character grows through,
unyielding perseverance, unrelenting grit, unflinching resilience,
and the insatiable pursuit
of insight, knowledge, and spirituality.

Out character is genuine only when we perennially put into practice,
inescapable forgiveness of oneself and others,
coupled with readiness
to rectify and learn from our mistakes.

Our character is revealed as to what we are really made of,
when demanded and required by life and its circumstances,
which may involve,
abnegation, sacrifice, and even relinquishment,
as the ultimate test about
the fiber, nature, and the substance our hearts are made of.

Our character perennially renews itself,
and remains crystalline
through unstained innocence, unpremeditated candor,
joyful spontaneity, and boundless ingenuity.

Our character builds a legacy with never ending and bountiful deeds,
empathetic and mindful judgment, unbreakable courage,
unwavering effort, undeterred resoluteness, relentless pace,
obsessive zeal, unwavering firmness, unleashed talent,
incomparable and unmatched ability, opportune impulsiveness,
and unfettered ingeniousness.

Our character transcends
when we are "ready to be" or "forever are"
in love with life, everyone, and our true love,
all with sustained passion.

Being alive presents us with countless paths
that in the pursuit of moral excellence,
elevate our character to its pinnacle,
engendering a state of <u>unrepentant virtuosity</u>.

"Snap"
(Snap out of It)

There are moments in life that overwhelm us,
they seize us right at the gut level,
suddenly we are crumbling inside,
without a clue,
how to cope with the situation.

Sometimes, it's simply doubting creeping in,
or anguish overwhelming our spirit
or just paralyzing cold fear.
Some others, the shell shock is much more profound
as we might be in pain or grieving a loss.

But in modern life though,
the prevailing catalysts are, pressure and stress,
induced by an ever-increasing overload,
coupled with a frantic and neurotic pace.

But, what about simply Snapping out of it!
Snap! Snap out of it!
Snap away from the moment,
freeze the picture around you,
freeze life's image,
just freeze it!
Separate yourself from the situation you are in.

Think only in nice, beautiful images, and let them take you over.

Focus on what you have, not on what is missing,
zero in on what you hold, not on what you lost,
then, dream about what you want,
visualizing yourself chasing it, with all your heart.

Snap out of it without fear,
do it without doubts,
remind yourself that quitting
does not exist in your vocabulary.

Snap away automatically when the situation arises,
without delay.

You have to catch these poisonous states, before they take a hold or spread.

Now relax.
Let go.
Contemplate the image you've frozen from the outside.
Then, as you decompress,
you'll realize, what your coping mechanisms are.

Did you focus on one thing and one thing only?
If so, then you snapped away through a meditative state.
Or did you simply do it by being aware
of the situation and separating yourself from it?
Or did you do it by freezing the moment?
Freezing the image? Freezing the picture?
Or did you do all of them by simply stepping back?
In the end how you did it,
matters only as to the path to take next time.

What is really important is that
you know now, how to snap out,
and how to snap away from the moment.
And you know now,
how to conquer life's circumstances,
before they conquer you.

"The Chimney Sweep"

The chimney sweep sits on a rooftop
of the city moonless night.

Stars by the millions gaze
like magnificent gatherings in the universe,
through luminescent eyes,
with infinite shades of white,
in full display,
just for him.

The sweep is done for the night.
The job thoroughly completed,
having uncluttered and unplugged,
the chimneys and spirits,
of the city dwellers.

Now he waits for the spectacle to begin.
Then, as the large metropolis falls asleep
with the gateways and launching pads prepared,
free of any debris or impediments,
the city and its people are ready to start dreaming.

So, it begins... First a few,
then an avalanche of people's dreams,
fly unimpeded,
out of countless chimneys into the night sky.

They are like projectiles flying straight
into the firmament of the universe,
taking away dreamer's dreams,
far into the limitless space,
toward the watchful eyes of millions of stars,
waiting for them.

"Faith"

Faith is a celestial force and a belief in outcomes
that we willfully invoke, to profess our credos
with overwhelming intensity.

Faith morphs believing
into an unstoppable inner strength
that becomes our spiritual engine
and dotes on us
a continuum of goodness and a giving soul.

Faith is awareness of the spirit and mindfulness of the soul.

Faith is the indispensable source of meaning in our lives.

Faith is mysterious as it deals
with two rational unsolvable existential questions:

The conundrum of creation,
and the enigma of a higher calling.

Faith is the realization
that even though there are many questions
about our universe's origin
we don't have an answer for
—neither do we have proof how it was created,
nor where will we be after life—
yet, we still deliberately chose
to believe wholeheartedly and steadfastly
in the existence of The Creator of it all.

Faith is unconditional love,
as well as,
the immutable,
unstoppable,
unwavering,
"unflickering,"

stubborn,
and indomitable belief
that there is a reason and a purpose for us being here,
dictated and gifted by The Creator.

When we profess it inside of a cocoon,
faith is nothing more
than an empty shell of falsehood.
Individualistic faith thrives
behind shields and walls of weakness,
erected to shy away,
disconnected from the world
through pitiful, self-serving beliefs,
just tunnel vision fantasies of our mind,
like mirages in the desert.

The world of darkness awaits us *when faith is blind*.
A life without a telescope may lead is into perilous paths
filled with dire and unintended consequences.

In the face of *misguided faith*,
life's vessel quickly loses its compass and purpose.
It becomes rudderless, without direction.
Thus, we are propelled forward by fake passions and beliefs,
into tumbling trajectories,
where, if our endeavors prove to be hazardous or hurtful,
faith becomes a runaway train
that inexorably derails, crashes, and burns.

To the contrary, *faith is authentic
when driven by virtue*, The Creator or both.
But we are not born in faith or virtue
as both have to be acquired, and they grow in tandem,
feeding off each other driven by our beliefs.

Faith ages well over time, like a good wine,
out of our relentless pursuit,
through hard work and discipline, of virtue, excellence,
and an inalterable and unassailable belief in The Creator of all things.

When we have faith,
We see light in darkness,
We give love when there is hate,
We offer compassion where there is suffering and pain,
We provide healing when there are wounds,
We show loyalty where there is betrayal,
We eagerly reconcile when there is conflict,
We readily forgive where there is hurt,
We sacrifice and abnegate for those that need it most.
We ascend and rise to the occasion,
when the circumstances could not be worse,
We acquiesce and adjourn when the situation requires it,
We are always austere and humble,
We are always grateful and anonymous in our actions,
while our heart is pure, crystalline, joyful and wholesome.
Above all, we blindly trust
what The Creator teaches and expects of us.

When we have faith,
we acclaim life and humanity,
elevating our existence to a higher calling,
One where we acquire through creed and conversion,
a noble purpose for the spirit,
and a God driven meaning for the soul.

"Whispering At Your Heart"

What is it that is so magnificent about you?

You are special because you are unique and inimitable.

You are magical because everything you touch
with your magic wand,
falls under a divine incantation.

You are beautiful as your heart is.
You are intense as your feelings are.

You are as driven and indomitable as your passions are.

You are as immutably firm as you are fiercely loyal.

You are made out of unwavering convictions and unbreakable beliefs.

You are tirelessly steady
because of your relentless discipline, perseverance,
and a consistency that never waivers or ceases to be.

You are sincere, genuine, and honest
because irrespective of what others think or say,
you always follow your heart.

You are built out of unlimited strength, courage, and integrity.
You are so valiant!
Again and again, you always defeat fear.

You are pretty in the morning, and even prettier at sundown.

You are genuine and adorable
because you're filled with innocence and candor.

You are noble and dependable
because rain or shine, wind, or heavy seas, you're always there.

You are virtuous and giving
because you are always ready to forgive and help others.

You are humble as you are quick to admit your faults
and make amends at lightning speed.

And you have this eternal halo doted on you by Heaven's angels,
an impenetrable shield,
protecting you against anything or anyone,
built out of unshakeable faith,
a steadfast character, a wholesome set of virtues,
and a fierce and relentless pursuit of excellence.

All of this and much more is you.
You are my life's journey companion,
Forever yours,
My love.

"Life, Evolution and change Among Us"

Two of the most fundamental and existential states in life
are measured by each stroke forward in our life clock's hands.

The corroboratory ticks
of the larger and faster ones
are those of the sounds of Change,
and the validating clicks
of the smaller and slower ones,
are those of the sounds of Evolution.

If the minutes tick,
then the hours will inevitably click as well.

Change engenders Evolution. Evolution provokes Change.

If Change is the transition from one condition to another,
then Evolution is a series of guided changes of advancement.

Change opens doors.
Evolution takes and keeps us inside.

Change occurs in the pursuit of
something new, different, perhaps disrupting.
Evolution is the outcome of such endeavors.

Change is the end of a paradigm.
Evolution is the new one.

Change requires willingness and desire.
Evolution is self-evident.

Change could trigger second chances.
Evolution is the second chance itself.

Awareness of Change is lasting and most effective
when rewarded by Evolution.

When Change is incremental,
Evolution validates it.

Change and Dogma mix like oil and water.
Evolution is the result of discarded dogma.

Change is easily measurable in magnitudes.
It can be seasonal and occurs in batches.
Evolution is easily quantifiable as well.
It is constant and transits throughout all seasons.

When we change for others our Heart reigns,
and Evolution is our new richer Royal Heart.

When Change is circumstantial,
the existence or lack of Evolution is incontrovertible evidence
whether Change is for better or worse.

Change is fruitful when driven by mindfulness.
Evolution is the fruit of such behavior.

Real Change requires truthfulness.
Evolution is the validation of such platitude.

When combined with greed and power,
monsters can be born out of Change.
Thus, instead of Evolution
we can regress backwards on a downward spiral.

Change can also be opportunistic and circumstantial
or rehearsed and deliberate,
but its execution and validation are essentially the same,
the old trusty tool of Evolution.

When we Change,
we willingly want to transfer, break, pass over, disrobe, mutate, alter,
modify, transform, convert, vary, substitute, exchange, replace, switch,
enhance a position or course, status, or state, depart from beliefs,

credos, or norms, deviate from character,
sequence or condition, insurge, diverge or shift.
It is only through Evolution that we execute them all.

Change is not constrained by time, but by opportune circumstances.
Evolution is the reward for proper timing.

Change is virtuous when driven by moral truisms,
and the choice of excellence.
Evolution is the actual acquisition of such altruism.

Change is observed, recognize, and valued
when not self-proclaimed or touted,
and the proof of such worthy behavior
lies in the presence or absence of Evolution,
as a consequence of our behavior.

As we are trepidatious about it,
Change requires courage and valor.
The resulting Evolution is our medal of honor.

Through Change and Evolution our life is never stagnant,
always moving forward,
constantly renewing itself
in a state of constant flux.

If we embrace Change,
we are in harmony and in accordance
with the laws of nature and the rules of life.
Welcoming one of our universal key dimensions,
that of a perennial and endless transformation.

The sounds of Change and the winds of Evolution
tick and click in sync,
inexorably forward, never swaying away.

Click-tick…Tick-click…Tick-tick…Click-click…

"Life Wizards"

If you want to find where our life wizards lie,
pay attention to those that have lived long,
and still possess candid and innocent hearts.

Their spirits are genuine, playful, and childlike,
their souls are gentle,
soaked in goodness and good faith,
their intent is always noble and transparent.

There is not even an iota
of malice or premeditation to be found in them.

Their personalities are made out of extraordinary attitudes
like spontaneity, ingenuity, inspiration,
and most of all,
love for life and its people.

These kind of life wizards laugh plenty and often out loud.
They smile at everyone and everything
whether silly or profound, or simply for no reason at all.

They are also giving and doting,
with boundless patience and tolerance.

They are always ready
to serve, help, assist, educate and rescue.
They are forever at the service of others.

They are humble and wise as well.
This allows them not to take anything or anyone too seriously,
always looking for the brighter side of people and things.

Fittingly, these whimsical and scintillating individuals
are not self-conscious at all about who they are.
Hence, our life's wizards are always defined by others
that spot and recognize them, throughout their lives.

They are also dependable and reliable.
Thus, they are the ones we seek to lean on,
providing us with safe harbor,
in the direst of circumstances.

These life sorcerers inhabit a land
where every moment and every person
are precious and irreplaceable.

Their reactions are measured,
always assuming good faith,
allowing the benefit of the doubt first.

Their benevolent, perennial sunny disposition
usually originates out of their strength of character,
the richness of their virtues and heart.

They also possess a flawless,
self-regulating "life compass"
allowing them to exercise impeccable judgment
causing noble reactions
regardless of situation or individuals.

These exceptional fellow life travelers
elevate themselves above the mundane, effortlessly.

Above all, their attitude towards life
shows us that no matter how long we've lived,
there are those that somehow
manage to filter and block out,
the poisons of the spirit, soul, and heart,
we encounter along the paths of life.

Life wizards are easy to identify
but difficult to value or live with for very long
as they inadvertently may make us feel inadequate.

That is precisely our challenge
-how to learn from and emulate these life sorcerers-
when their intense inner lights
may make ours seem opaque and dark.

So, pay attention to these champions of life
that know how to keep everything in balance,
and find everyone and everything priceless.

Pay attention and take advantage
of these exceptional fellow life companions
—life wizards—
as they possess the magic formula of how to live a happy life
while preserving a candid and innocent heart,
for those old souls
are not frequently found.

"Life As A Journey"

We travel through life
from the moment we arrive on planet Earth.

Wherever we are, whatever we do,
we are always going somewhere
as there's always a destination.

But the journey is where our life resides,
not the destination.

In so many ways,
life is a magnificent, vast, perilous ocean.

Our journey is the path we follow,
the wake we leave behind,
accompanied by fellow travelers joining us along the way,
and we are the vessels sailing though it all.

Of all our fellow travelers, some are better than others.
With many we have a choice with others we don't.
Some are with us for good,
others drop off along the way.
But, our closest, most loyal, and beloved companions,
are those whose presence stays with us forever.

Our life's vessel is sturdy and resilient.
If in addition,
we trust it, know it, maintain it,
conduct it, will it, and love it well,
our ship will be able to withstand and endure
virtually any rogue wave or weather any storm,
life throws at us.

Life's journeys occur because we seek to travel,
throughout the earth's seas,
in knowledge and expectation,

that there are endless places to be discovered,
and innumerable fellow travelers
we may meet our encounter along the way.

There are moments in life
when we soar above the oceans,
and there are others,
when we drop all the way to the bottom.

As in life,
on an ocean voyage we reach countless ports of call,
some picture perfect,
others filled with trappings,
some with rocky shores
or dangerous landings.
Sometimes sandy beaches await us,
some others our destination is unbearable
and demands high sacrifices.

On occasion the seas are calm.
the gentle breeze allows for smooth sailing,
on those precious days the sun is gentle,
the rain is just a drizzle.

Sometimes the oceans display happiness and joy.
On such days, the sounds of the sea
feel like a magnificent concerto,
with every instrument playing the inspiring music of life,
with the sky painted in glorious colors and tones.
In these moments,
we seemingly float or walk over water,
we ride the waves,
kite the wind,
ski the surface
or dive under it.

On these days we rejoice,
celebrate the oceans

and life's voyage is a joyful ride,
that we wish would never cease to be.

But there are instances when we can barely swim
or even stay afloat
as the heavy seas try to drag us down
with their heaviest ballasts.

On those days,
the oceans seemingly weep in pain,
flailing against the rocks,
and the skies drum and lament
in opaque colors of sorrow.

During those moments,
all seems full of sadness and nostalgia,
yet we resist, vanquish,
and get to live another day.

Sometimes when we are hit by weather systems,
more often than not,
after the fact,
we come to the realization that preparation,
prudence and alertness,
could or would've prevented it all.

Thus, Life's grand travail can be rough and trying.
The ocean's natural elements
may show us their force and strength
as if there was anger and fury,
bursting out of them.

When this happens,
we fight and conquer
By seeking to endure, overcome and outlast them.

When the oceans flip into monsters in an instant,
their waves become voracious destructors
of anything in sight.

Hence, there are no autopilots in life,
neither can we take for granted at any time,
the safe passage of our vessel.

That is why, on a well-travelled life journey,
we appreciate and value the good days against the bad ones,
as we know that the latter will come, sooner or later.

On the voyage of life, we will experience,
birth and love,
death and hope,
triumph and defeat,
faith, and doubt,
wonder and awe,
magic, and reality,
construction, destruction and reconstruction,
genius, and talent,
laughter and tears,
mediocrity, and tireless efforts,
celebration and mourning,
fame and repudiation,
truth and falsehood,
health, and pain,
betrayal and forgiveness,
tragedy and renewal,
passion and humbleness,
failure, and redemption,
and they will come to us
on all kinds of days, weathers, and seas.

As the journey moves along,
we will learn again and again that only
love,
faith,
courage,
experience,
knowledge,
and hope
will see us through the rough patches.

Life's circles are in fact a journey
we travel endlessly nonstop,
soaring above or struggling underneath,
through calm or high seas,
through rain or sunshine,
through countless ports of call.

And we ride,
along with travel companions that join us along the way.
We journey relentlessly,
from beginning to end,
through the oceans of life,
with a restless spirit,
and a gypsy soul.

"Of Wealth, Fame and Love"

In one way or another,
we all chase, some of us relentlessly,
Wealth, Fame, and Love,
in this exact order of importance.

But these life illusions
don't always present themselves
in such a prescribed pecking order.

Fact is,
we never know who shows up first,
or if any of them will ever make itself present at all.

But if they do,
we will face one of life's most puzzling conundrums,
that is, what we are keenly after,
is not only elusive,
but usually comes
at the expense of something else.

Correspondingly, more often than not,
when we are graced with riches and a good name,
it comes at the expense of love,
or if we become wealthy,
it's at the expense of the other two,
or a good reputation comes without love or riches,
or love blesses us without riches or even a good name.

What is not so apparent though,
is that this mirage triad of grand illusions,
we covet so much,
comes at the expense of other, even more important virtues,
- some existential in nature, others, crucial life attitudes -
than our three grand illusory obsessions.

As we chase wealth, we sacrifice frugality,
and run the risk of losing our ability to appreciate
the true value of people or material things,
or perhaps even worse
we may become unable
to value the simplest of things,
especially those that are nominally scarce
in quantifiable magnitudes.

As we go after reputation, we run the risk
that nothing about us is nameless any longer,
and the fiction of what others think about us,
morphs into an obsession,
becoming more important
than the reality of who we really are.

Falsely, anonymity then becomes
a synonym for failure or lack of accomplishment,
and everything we do, or we work for,
becomes attached to our name and ego.

But the biggest risk we face chasing fame
is that everything we do in life,
for others or ourselves,
becomes somewhat and somehow,
driven, and conditioned by what others think,
how they react
and how they behave.
Causing us to lose part of our sense of identity,
as the purest of all acts in life,
the acts of conscience,
where we are only accountable to ourselves,
totally escape us.

But the most difficult
of our life's grand illusions to go after is love
as by doing so,
we run the risk of sacrificing freedom.

Love is a compromise between two souls,
where each one "gives in" a part of themselves,
and a couple is born.
A twosome is a separate unit from the two individuals though,
and the balance between
the individuality of each one versus the couple,
even though attainable,
is very difficult to achieve,
even more so to maintain.

The dilemma lies in,
that self-determination and liberty
are not that compatible with love.
It takes a lot of maturity, tolerance, and compromise
for both to coexist.

It is perhaps in true love
where the boundaries within a couple blend best.
This happens,
when freedom instead of being an obstacle,
is actually the bond
that unites authentic love.
Strings and ties,
are not driven by walls of insecurity and possession,
but by the natural, spontaneous, comfortable
yearning for our other half
and the certainties of immanent belonging to someone else's heart.

Are we then just chasing,
these three grand illusions in life?
Is this all we are capable to do?
Are they only a mirage?
Do we sacrifice frugality and austerity
when we go after riches and wealth?
Do we lose anonymity and our own identity
when we are after reputation and a good name
Do we lose freedom and self-determination
when we join in love?

Before chasing wealth,
perhaps we should learn first to be frugal and austere,
in order to learn the true value of things,
and how precious each fellow human being is.

And we should learn how to be humbly anonymous and
modestly nameless first,
doing things for ourselves,
based on our conscience alone,
before chasing reputation and a good name,
which are always based
on what others think of us,
instead of, what we really think about ourselves.

And we could learn about
freedom and self-determination first,
hopefully before true love finds us,
hooking us up with someone else,
so, we will be capable of balancing the emerging
couple with our individuality and sense of being.

Life is a mirage of three grand illusions,
Wealth, Fame, and Love,
requiring a fine balance between them,
as not to hurt some,
at the expense of a triad of others,
namely, Frugality, Anonymity, and Freedom as
we require them as well,
for a wholesome, well balanced and happy life.

"Of Family, True Friendship and Love"

In all matters of family, true friendship, and love,
reside all of those that are dearest and nearest to us,
as well as the bonds that hold them together.

The tight closeness and indivisible unity
of these three existential bonds
are one of the most important sources
of strength and happiness in our lives.

We can never be careful enough though, as once the
closeness and tightness
of these bonds is lost,
it is extremely trying, and difficult to recover them.

That is why,
we always defend and protect our walls of intimacy.
Closeness and tightness are not immanent,
they have to be earned
through daily work and sacrifices
that we pour into
our family, true friends and loved ones.

The source of the power and strength of these bonds,
originates out of sticking together as a whole,
irrespective of anything or anyone.

Happiness and joy ensue,
from the intimacy and closeness of living in full,
along with those we love or who are dear to us.

All of our actions,
regarding our family, true friendship and loved ones
are driven by acts of conscience,
where we are first accountable to ourselves, and act driven by it,
not because we are conditioned or limited
by what those closest to us do, say, or think.

However,
the boundaries between,
what we must do,
what is expected of us,
and vice versa,
in matters of the heart, true friendship, and family,
are at best tenuous,
more than likely moving targets
or even shifting sands.

Unless we are willing and able
to formulate and enunciate a declaration,
in a way a manifesto that dresses us with a sacred
mantle comprised of these precious existential bonds,
while at the same time casting in stone
with sufficient clarity,
what is it exactly that we pursue and aspire?

It reads as follows:

Together,
We love unlimitedly with all our hearts,
are fiercely and infinitely loyal,
always pursue and preserve unity,
conduct ourselves with impeccable dignity,
defend and maintain the integrity of our honor,
incessantly and humbly pray in the practice of our faith,
treasure each and every precious memory and moment,
never surrender the power of hope,
never, ever leave unfinished business,
neither quit, jump ship, abandon, run away, waver, flicker, brake ranks
or voluntarily leave anyone behind.

To preserve one another
we are ready and will walk on fire.

And if we fail, we fail together,
but always rebound and get back-up,
again and again, again and again.

Then,
As life's paths and careers brew
unfolding into tangible efforts of personal growth,
deliberate undertakings
or simply, projects under way.
We nurture,
prepare, support, exalt, motivate, believe in, assist, lift, cheer,
set, guide, tender, advice, steer, stick with, cling,
inspire, role model, praise, teach with endless patience,
and are always there,
available at any time when we are needed.

In other circumstances,
when we are required to intervene
we get involved swiftly and decisively,
we confront, level with, admonish, claim to, protest to,
complain about, refute, dissent from, contradict, oppose,
prevent, save, avoid, change directions from, rectify,
listen well and even if within our grasp, forbid outright.

On other occasions,
when we are tested inside out,
our virtues and values,
especially our integrity and capacity to give,
are challenged to extremes.
Those moments,
We hoist high up the shiny flag of the truth,
have above all, boundless patience,
are always ready to respond,
have sound tolerance for, offer generous wisdom to,
behave with compassion for,
act with composure and moderation for,
are ready to give and share what we have,
dependably fulfilling all our promises and commitments,
always respecting and valuing others.

When we err or make mistakes:
We are contrite, make amends,
repent, seek atonement for,
are always ready to forgive and be forgiven.

Etiquette, decorum, and true respect
are not only expected but also required from all of us,
therefore, we never,
yell, curse, shout, scream, humiliate, insult, derogate,
hurt, sink, diminish, put down, seek revenge,
judge, or criticize others.

We seek to be a role model by being perennially humble.
Thus,
We pursue frugality, modesty, discretion, and moderation.

Breeding the new generations is part of our duties,
Hence,
We always provide, train, teach, hold accountable, inculcate,
assign responsibility, and invest in one another.

But above all,
We never lose perspective about the simple things in life.
Therefore, sweet, or painful, we always tell the truth.
We laugh and enjoy, smile, and have fun,
rejoice and share happiness.

And together we acclaim, celebrate, and enjoy a life of
Family, True Friendship and Love.

"One Verse At Poet's Row"

As the leaves drop at Poet's row,
I see your eyes sparkle in the hues of the fall.

The gentle breeze whistles
as the spirit of "The Big Apple"
spreads to every corner
of the city's lungs.

The park is colored with captivating tones
of endless yellows and oranges
and why not?
bits of red as well,
seemingly all,
just for you,
my love.

It is in this hallowed corner
where your smile shines the most,
as your head full of dreams realizes,
that your heart has been taken,
on an autumn's romance,
by the spirit of the park
and by my very own,
while I recite this verse
made out of precious fallen leaves,
and my infatuated heart and soul,
succumbing all to you my love,
right here at Poet's Row.

"Life As A Circus"

Life is like a circus
with the exact same cast of characters
popping out of its book pages.

We are surrounded by "ring masters"
pulling all the strings, building, and running civilization.

We find the "acrobats"
like equilibrists or trapezists
that defy gravity
performing jaw dropping pirouettes
as part of their daily lives.

We marvel at the "magicians" and "illusionists"
who make us believe
in what is apparently not real
through their ability
to dream, visualize,
enhance, or augment mundane reality.
And some of them actually dare to,
and make it a true reality,
causing incremental quantum leaps
for the advancement and evolution of society.

We stumble into "jugglers"
who master dexterity and multi-tasking
as if was second nature to them,
in order not only
to meet the challenges of a complex world,
but more importantly,
to be the ones who assemble, operate,
and maintain the engines of civilization.

We rely "the lion and tiger tamers"
to control the wild and uncivilized,
the rule breakers,

in order to maintain social order and peace,
through the enforcement
of the laws of men.

We seek the "sword swallowers" and "fire eaters"
who defy danger and death
with each and every move or throw,
we usually hand them the controls
putting out lives in their hands
because we trust their skills
and their endless rehearsal and preparation,
to deliver us safely to our destination,
as their feats don't allow
for a single false step, or bad move.

We run across the "cannon ball men"
who like to live life on a bang,
for them the flights to nowhere
are the high they need and seek.
For these flights,
they are willing to take life to the limit,
just to fly for a few seconds,
even though their trajectories
inevitably always end,
in a crash and burn situation.

We enjoy the "clowns and jesters"
always after a practical joke or a roast,
whether is through ridicule,
outrageousness or burlesque.
They are perennially chasing
the lighter side of things,
in pursuit of laughter or a smile,
of which there are never enough in life.

Be being the "spectators and patrons"
We get to witness and approve, or disapprove
of everything that takes place
during the show in a ring.

We are demanding and judgmental.
As an intelligent herd,
We never miss a beat,
and sometimes even alter,
the very acts of a life in a circus.

Same as children never forget
their first time at the circus,
the biggest show on Earth,
appeals to the inner child in all of us as well,
this occurs because in the circus
we witness the show of life
without prejudice,
social rules filters,
or the arrest of the mundane.

The circus' spectacle displays performers
in the exercise of their best talents,
candidly exposed,
executing stunning acts,
that even though rehearsed to perfection,
are so daring, and outrageous,
even seemingly impossible,
that we rave in childlike exuberance.

As we do in life,
circus performers
come from all walks of life,
and they all have something in common,
spectators recognize and covet.
They do what they love,
and what they are passionate about.

Circus performers achieve their high standards
through exceptional drive and desire,
innate abilities and strenuous preparation
over extended periods of time.

We find circus performers,
on every corner of the streets of life,
not only as shiny artists, and elite athletes,
but also, as common citizens,
willing to tap their full potential
by pursuing what they are good at.

We all have a bit or much
of these characters inside each one of us.
What is it?
A bit of a clown mixed with a full-blown illusionist?
Or a bit of a trapezist combined with a full-blown juggler?
Or perhaps a bit of a ring master
blended with a full-blown clown?

Whoever is the circus character that fits us best,
fact is,
in the characters of the circus
reside some of our best talents and strengths.

In the characters of a circus,
we get to contemplate, and appreciate
what happens?
When we tap our full potential.

Life is a circus,
in as much as,
we let out inner child rejoice and embrace
its own characters,
without filters, fears, or prejudice,
in order to discover which one
or several of them is us.
So, we can unleash and soar
through the best use of our talents and passions,
like true circus performers do.

"Those Shiny Curls of Mine"

The gentle breeze tussles freely,
those shiny curls of mine.

The vast ocean reflects
a magnificent canvas
to draw into eternity
those incandescent eyes
that I belong to,
now and forever.

With a cornucopia
of blues, silvers, and whites,
I am handed the privilege
of an endless palette,
to paint your gorgeous smile
that now owns me whole,
with no room to spare,
but just for our two big hearts,
tightly bundled together,
loving each other to no end.

On one side of the horizon,
the sun rises
bringing soft, bright hues of light
to the new day,
and along with it,
an aura of ethereal beauty
to your morning self,
one I contemplate in awe and wonder
and wish it to be as well,
only mine.

Simultaneously,
on the other side of the horizon,
the sun sets
with intense tones,
same as your passions and fires,

to those I surrender forever.
Through them
my heart is completely yours,
and no longer mine.

And on the middle of the horizon
as a backdrop
to our sails and craft,
displaying every color
there is in our universe,
sits an extraordinary rainbow,
traversing the skies in full
from end to end,
framing you at the center
into a perennial pose,
with your gorgeous smile,
incandescent eyes
and the gentle sea breeze
tussling freely
those beautiful, shining, curls of mine.

"Clarity in Life"

Those that regret in never ending fashion,
and those that drown in their sorrows
seemingly forever,
lack clarity in life.

Craving for an alternative reality
of "what ifs" "what could or should have been"
is a fruitless search
for a time machine,
or an alternative reality or dimension
that simply do not exist.

Lamenting past events, difficulties, even tragedies
on endless loops of pain,
leaves us stuck, infinitely drowning, or gasping for air.

Regrets and sorrows are fueled and driven
by deeply ingrained insecurities, fear and guilt,
with all of them working as magnifying glasses
distorting and exaggerating true pain and real losses.

Regrets and sorrows take us to places
where we end up with whom we don't like or love,
or doing what we don't want,
or longing for people and things we no longer have or never did,
or simply don't exist any longer.

Material wealth is a source for freedom from poverty
but is not a substitute for fear, guilt, shortcomings,
false aspirations, or the void of emptiness of spirit and soul.

Riches are not only existentially worthless,
and mislead us into a false sense of security,
but they are also another source
for future states of loneliness, regret, and sorrow.

We have clarity in life,
when instead of craving, we aspire.
Instead of wanting what we don't have, or already lost,
we dream, visualize, and strive
how to procure it or get it back.

We have clarity in life,
when we have a clear purpose,
and constantly search for meaning.

We have clarity in life,
when we are fully aware of our strengths and weaknesses,
when we constantly and relentlessly,
seek to build a wholesome set of virtues,
and when we are fully aware of,
which of those virtues we've already acquired,
then strive to put them into action.

We have clarity in life
when we conduct ourselves with responsibility,
while exercising judicious discipline.

We have clarity in life
when we invariably seek, accept, defend, and protect the truth.

When we achieve clarity in life,
we are graced with redemption to our fallings,
through the power of our faith and beliefs,
under the mantle of trust.

We have clarity in life,
when we understand that we can always reinvent ourselves,
and move forward without breaking our core,
following our convictions with unyielding fashion
and when we treasure true love,
using it as our source of happiness and inspiration.

Clarity in life inexorably leads
to accomplishment and self-confidence,
which in turn lead us to virtuous circles,
where regrets and sorrows have no place to be,
nor any air to breath.

Clarity opens life for us,
expanding our horizons,
leaving no limits in the sky before us,
an endless firmament,
and the living universe
for us to experience, enjoy and appreciate.

"Contemplating Your Face"

Over time our faces become a reflection of our lives,
and what we are made of, inside.

Over time the mask of our youth fades away
as we bear the marks and scars of the kind,
and way of life we've lived or experienced.

In a well-weathered face,
like a fingerprint,
every little crevice, corner, ridge, or wrinkle
coming out of our unguarded rictuses,
and spontaneous gestures,
reflect our deeds, our highs, and lows,
our wins, losses and defeats, our pain and joy,
-in plain sight and exposed for all to see-
like signage,
and there's nothing we can do to hide them.

Does our face look deeply angry?
What about mean-spirited?
Perhaps artificial?
Or does it exude goodness, nobility,
a gentle spirit, and an inspired soul?
Does it show darkness, and solitude or optimism and enthusiasm?
Does it vibe anguish and sadness or happiness and joy?
Does it show depression and despair or cheerfulness and passion?
Whatever your honest answer is, that's likely who you are.

But nothing in our face,
conveys more about our true nature, and human condition,
than our eyes.

There are those that are downright scary
as they portray death
from those that have made contact with it,
for the right or wrong reasons.

Others depict madness
and we can sense the tumultuous,
unsettled internal world of the person we face.

What about,
those that are simply empty,
and there is no one home.

In life we find an endless gallery
within the human species
—the envious eyes, the obsessed, ambitious,
vengeful, sad, angry, resentful, greedy or hypocrite.

In contrast to those
that are, gentle, benign, giving, doting, inspiring, healing, happy,
joyful, patient, grateful, forgiving or simply glorious,
outright awesome, incandescent, twinkling, even magical.

Then, there is love.
Our eyes and faces are transformed under the mantle of love.
Youth, freshness, rosiness, sparkle, and glow,
cover us with a halo projecting luminescent-positive energy,
impregnated with enchanting, contagious vitality.

The look of love is a masterpiece,
where we see drawn on our loved ones
all we share and treasure with them.

That's why,
when we contemplate the faces of our life partners,
we see well beyond what anyone else could,
as every move, each angle, every sight,
reflects a different moment of a life together.

Each expression and gesture remind us
of a different anecdote, circumstance,
or life experience with them.

We place their laughters on eternal memories, we
vividly remember their smiles
on countless occasions, places,
and we see their tears of joy or sadness
as those we shared
and experienced as a couple.

We see in flashes drawn on their faces,
the movie of our life journey,
like the first time we discovered
our life partners maternal or paternal eyes,
when our children were born,
or their eyes of sadness on each of our departures
followed by the bursts of joy,
and relief upon our safe returns.

Or their gestures of disgust
at our transgressions or disappointments,
or their immense happiness
when their hearts were taken by surprise by spontaneous gestures,
heartfelt little details
or even a tiny single flower.

When we see that face
That's journeyed with us for so long,
we see every little thing
that is as much a part of us as it is of theirs.

That is how we can't help but to contemplate
—unwittingly, and to a degree unknowingly, —
in awe and wonder,
the unique kind of beauty
that is made out of the richness,
of a joined life story,
filled with countless,
and unforgettable mementos.

That is the reason
no one can appreciate, and value or understand,
read, see, or fully feel better
our life's partner's eyes and faces, than us,
simply because only we know,
and have experienced,
the life story and anecdotes behind them.

"Gratitude"

The most important forms of gratitude
are either celestial
or existential in nature.

Enough has been professed, and predicated, describing Gratitude.

Yet, its essence does not lie in the WHAT?
It resides in the WHEN, WHY, AND HOW.

We are truly grateful
when we are Selfless in our gestures and expectations.

We are genuinely grateful on our actions
If we are keenly aware of its existential and imperative necessity:
Such as to perennially reciprocate,
and give back to life and others,
for the privilege of being alive.

For Gratitude to be authentically proffered or conveyed.
For Gratitude to resonate, or be empathetic.
It requires the virtues of Humility, and Respect.

Selflessness, Awareness, Humility, and Respect
are the essence of
WHEN, WHY AND HOW?
Gratitude takes place.

Our mere existence is inexplicably fortunate, immensely blessed.
For it, we thank our Creator
for ordaining us into this universe,
instead of the trillions of other reproductive cells,
that never make it through
the procreation, and gestation stages, preceding birth.

Once we arrive though,
we have much to be grateful for,
certainly for every day
we are alive, healthy, conscious,
and surrounded by friends and family.
But alongside these two, is our Gratitude for others.

In Gratitude,
We recognize the loyalty others demonstrate to us.
In Gratitude,
We value the faith others maintain on us.
In Gratitude,
We acknowledge the worthiness of one another's gestures.
In Gratitude,
We pay our respects as human beings
to those that dote on us whether we deserve it or not.
In Gratitude,
We reattribute with love, the love received.
In Gratitude,
We reward the acts of kindness we are graced with.
In Gratitude,
We enjoy what we give far more than what we receive.
In Gratitude,
We celebrate the naive and candid side of life.

Gratitude is most impactful
when it genuinely comes from the heart,
without the interference of ego, or social rules.
Genuine Gratitude does not expect anything in return.

Genuine Gratitude is spontaneous,
not dictated by anything, or anyone.

Genuine gratitude is anonymous,
it is just an act of our conscience.

Genuine Gratitude uplifts
who or what we are grateful for,
first, at the forefront,
while we remain behind the scenes.

Genuine Gratitude is never
proportionate or measurable in magnitudes.

Genuine Gratitude is expressed
through acts of love, gestures,
and even sacrifices.

To the contrary, false Gratitude
is a narcissistic farce,
as our only real concern is ourselves and our image,
not anyone else's.

Gratitude is a dependable source
of inner peace, happiness, and inspiration,
as its musical notes sing
to the better side of our human condition,
where the spark of creativity,
and visualization can be ignited in an instant,
triggering one of the noblest of all conditions,
that of being perennially thankful
to the Creator, for life, and to others.

"Always There"

Today my heart looked for you,
and I sighted in joy and relief,
as one more time,
when I needed it,
my dream of you,
was still there.

Somehow, I'd expected it to vanish,
but that's just the other side of me,
the one that tries to keep me grounded,
not letting me go anywhere.

Tonight, I went to bed early,
and your dream of me,
remained exactly where you left it,
right there.

Tomorrow, I'll be up before dawn
and shortly after, at sunrise,
our dream will make itself present,
as it perennially does,
always there.

"A Good Riddle"

A good riddle is hard to crack,
inevitably though,
They always have a solution.
Same for a puzzle, or a mystery.

But life is not always a riddle to be solved,
as its solutions
don't come in the form of passwords,
as more often than not
they are created or simply change or evolve
along the way.

Hence, even though life's riddles,
are always there to be solved,
their solutions are not
necessarily already there.

And if one has to be too careful
about what to ask for,
then some of life's riddles
are better left unresolved.

"Doubt"

A Doubt without Trust, Method, or Purpose
sets us up for recurring anxiety and pain,
unfortunately in vain,
as all of it will go to waste,
when inexorably,
we fail.

On these types of vacillations,
when in doubt, we are hiding something,
and doubts are just false shield and excuses
for the real roots and genesis of our behavior,
namely, weakness of character, lack of knowledge,
shortcomings on ability or talent,
lack of preparation or planning,
among others.

These types of indecisiveness,
seeks to justify mediocrity and incompetence,
through blaming or suspicions of others,
when in all likelihood, all what is wrong,
lies only within ourselves.

These types of hesitations,
are like deadly poison,
inevitably leading to inaction and paralyzing fear
as we are increasingly overwhelmed
by uncertainty, skepticism, apprehension,
and a nagging lack of confidence
that inexorably leads to errors in judgment.

This is the main reason why these types of doubts
are the telltale signs of failure.

The antidotes to doubting
are Trust, Method, and Purpose.

When we doubt, and apply Trust,
we resolve it
by giving the benefit of the doubt
to the person or situation.

We apply Method,
when we are objectively uncertain,
our inclination not to believe,
can be overruled by the observation of facts,
when we have uncertainty about our beliefs or opinions,
we can overcome them by curing
our incomplete knowledge or our lack of evidence.

We apply Purpose
when we are on an emotional overload,
under siege,
by avalanches of indecision.
We dissolve and break through them,
if, as we discard the waste,
we can keep our end game in sight,
or in case we realize we don't have such,
then we eagerly develop one,
as Purpose is the ultimate doubt breaker.

In final analysis,
a healthy dose of doubt
is an essential component of a wholesome life.

But it is our challenge,
in order to embrace doubt, to do it always
with <u>Trust, Method, or Purpose</u>.

"Duality"

Here is the problem with Duality:
At first sight seems to be something it isn't,
like a state of deliberate indecisiveness,
or even ignorant, willful duplicity,
amongst choices.

Duality is quite the contrary of what it appears to be,
at least as far as this verse goes...

We stumble into duality in life
when, either we crave, not one,
but the totality of choices ahead of us,
or we see everything, and everyone
as a two-sided proposition of "either or."

Not enough has been said about the first kind of duality,
consisting of the capricious art of wanting it both ways in life,
the art of wanting it all simultaneously, and at any cost,
no matter what, where, who, when, why or how.

This usually leaves no room for anything or anyone else.
This voraciousness, in most cases is in itself a problem,
not only because we seldom enjoy either one,
but also, because in addition,
malignant-greedy-duality,
is nothing but a pernicious existential waste of time,
a pointless, and fruitless
exercise in instant and constant gratification,
which is not only banal, empty, and not everlasting
but above all, devoid of any meaning and purpose,
hence not transcendental,
meaning that,
we are not "living" nor "alive"
when we practice it or chase it.

On the other hand,
when duality is polarizing,
we see the universe, the world, life, and its people
through opposing extremes,
with everything in between,
the antagonizing sides,
as irreconcilable differences all of the time.

Everything around us becomes,
black or white, good or evil, exhilarating or angsty,
fulfilling or empty, happy, or depressive,
crowded or lonely, entertaining or boring,
truthful or false, faithful or treasonous, and real or fake.

Everyone we interact with becomes,
either superior or lesser, affluent, or deprived, healthy,
or unwell, successful or a failure, entitled or a parasite,
solvent or a social ballast, with or against us,
able or handicapped, free or condemned,
innocent or scarlet-letter bearers,
low in self-esteem or narcissistic,
socially adequate or psychopaths.

Our emotional and rational lives are either,
controlled or chaotic, effusive or filled with resentment,
exuberant or frustrated, on a high or on a low, abstinent or viced,
carnivorous or vegan, nice or nasty,
generous, or greedy and selfish.

The shining light of lasting beauty of life,
lies not on opposite sides,
but right down the middle.
A wholesome life is driven by virtues,
residing strictly, and solely between extremes.
They're located in the area of confluence,
where we ponder and tinker,
with all our existential levers.

Instead of a world of pairs or duos,
or either "a" or "b" choices,
we find a third alternative,
made entirely out of both extremes.

That's where and how,
life can be brought into balance,
and why,
it's only in the middle where most,
if not all our existential virtues can be found:
Namely, temperance, uniqueness, out of the norm,
prudence, good judgment, patience, endurance,
tolerance, forgiveness, a good heart, creativity, artistry,
open mindedness, clarity, cautiousness,
meditative and contemplative states, repentance,
generosity, gratitude, moderation, hope, inspiration, frugality,
faith, change, evolution, our conscience,
our spirit, and our soul.

Duality by nature
is incomplete and unfulfilling
as it deprives us of all of the available choices,
sending us into extremes,
as well as,
absolute and utterly rigid positions.

Duality can be dangerous,
casting opposite or extreme sides against each other,
creating potential, or real conflicts
and clashes between the antagonizing parties,
based on the simple "diminimous" desire,
of one side prevailing over the other
at any and all costs.

Duality also casts blindness in our hearts, spirits, and souls,
depriving us of the ability to experience life,
and enjoy the universe, the world, nature,
and others simply because we ignore the third choice,
that of contemplating life half-way through extremes,
right down the middle.

"Geniality"

If we are content
to oversimplify what Geniality is,
limiting ourselves
to mean it as something
simply cordial, affable, congenial, gracious,
sociable, cheerful, and kindly,
we rob the uniqueness,
and outstanding aspects of its application.

Worst of all,
we trivialize the genius in all of us
which is an "intrinsical" part
of our essence and our sense of being.
Hence,
the Geniality we speak about in this scribble,
is such that comes out of genius.

Here's the contradictory problem with genius,
we haven't figured it out yet;
What is it mean to be a genius?
How is it to be genial, act genially,
possess genialness and geniality?
What is it to be able to genialize
ourselves, everyone, and everything we touch?

The fact is,
there's Geniality inside each one of us,
it resides somewhere within,
and it is eager and ready,
to be discovered, nurtured, developed,
exploited, and put into practice.

In a way, it's like our Geniality is a genie in a bottle.
However, we make it really hard to become genial.
We think of genial
in terms of the most exceptional, exclusive, and limited.

The absence of geniality
as less, common or everybody else.
We think of people, things in a binary way, up or down.
Geniuses are neither of them.

In fact, quite the contrary,
genialness to begin with,
levels the playing field.
Everyday geniuses do not feel better or less than others,
it's simply a term that does not exist in their dictionaries.

A genius is simply someone, anyone, everyone
that has recognized, discovered, or found
in himself or others,
all the talents and abilities
he was or others were born with,
and has uncorked, liberated, and implemented them.

A genius does not think in terms of being better,
and the rest of others being less than him.
He is simply really good at what he does best. Period.

Geniality can be found
where we hold innate, unlimited, and notable talent.
Any of us are genial,
when we're able to tap into our maximum potential,
using our best strengths.
At such moments we get to use our superpowers,
becoming masters of our genial potential.

But don't ever confuse this with simplicity
as genius only deals with hard challenges.
Nothing geniality tackles comes easy,
it's just that it looks that way from the outside,
in the hands of genial powers,
rehearsed talents, and well-trained abilities.

Ask yourself,
What am I really, really good at?
What was I born and destined to be?

What is it that I am passionate about and really love to do?
Honestly, what is it?
Given my abilities, passions, and talents,
what is it that I do best in life?
And if I haven't yet discovered it,
let me make it my life quest to find it.

One thing is certain,
the genius in all of us does not reside
where we don't have the talent,
and the passion to indulge into it.

The main obstacle and problem
with approaching geniality though,
is that it can be intimidating.
Thus, instead of embracing and getting
close, we shy away from it.

In actuality what we need to do is just the opposite.
In order to elevate ourselves,
we have to be exposed and surrounded by people
that have talents and abilities that are simply better than ours,
or that we aren't that accomplished or experienced at,
or simply haven't discovered yet.

The absence of Geniality occurs,
when envying the virtues and strengths of others,
we embark on the futile, poisonous exercise
of comparing ourselves to them,
often even worse, when we do it against the backdrop
of our most notorious weaknesses and shortfalls.

Geniality is always confused
as being solely the spectrum of those
with extraordinary native intellectual power,
transcendental mental superiority,
or amazing inventiveness, and ability.

Geniuses are perceived as profoundly gifted individuals
with attributes so diverse, complex and sophisticated.
We feel overwhelmed,
and out of step in front of them.

The question we have to ask ourselves in those instances is:
Are we afraid?
Do we feel inadequate and intimidated by extraordinary genius?
Or are we're just afraid of ourselves?

In this respect,
it's always healthy to remind ourselves
that, whatever someone else has,
we all have something different
but equally valuable in the universe of life.
It's also worth remembering that,
although we are all geniuses at one or a few things,
where we shine and soar,
we are all clumsy clowns on many, many others.

Hence, the genius in us does not compare
with anyone or anything,
because this is not only pointless,
but a zero-sum game
as our humbling flaws are always waiting for us,
on every corner of the streets of life.

So, what are we waiting for?
Our Geniality awaits us.
Our genie in a bottle is ready to be unlocked and liberated.
Let us unleash the genius inside all of us,
so, we can perform at our maximum potential
and at the top of our abilities
while being the best we can be in life.

"Adversity"

Either by acts of men, nature, or humanity's creations,
fatefully, sooner or later,
weather systems will gather in the horizon,
or events will happen unexpectedly.

Inevitably,
one way or another
with or without warning,
Adversity will hit us during our life's journey.

Adversity will affect us
emotionally, spiritually, physically, materially,
in any combination.

As a consequence,
when we face hardship in life,
there is no choice,
with impetus we gather
all our strengths, forces, and powers.
Those that we have,
those that we don't,
those that we reach from,
then go and face Adversity head on.

We confront Adversity for us, others, or both
without fear or hesitation,
with all our will and desire.

We aim at Adversity's bullseye,
seeking to live and overcome it.

Against Adversity,
we seek to raise back up, prevail, defeat,
rendering it completely annihilated, and vanquished.

When we don't confront
or face Adversity head on,
we find ourselves trapped
in a maze of indecisiveness,
drawing pointless circles within our minds,
while wasting valuable time,
avoiding or delaying action.

These are moments,
some lasting a lifetime,
where we find ourselves lamenting,
feeling sorry for ourselves or others,
procrastinating, commiserating, regretting,
while doing very little to fight back.

When we behave in such ways,
our failure to act leads us to nowhere,
except for reaching an empty place,
where eventually, all our excuses sound hollow,
not only robbing us of our ability to live in full,
but also reflecting the attitude of a soldier,
that runs away from the battle of life,
without ever firing a single shot,
as he is unwilling to face the enemy of Adversity
with the courage and conviction needed
to defeat it, or perhaps adapt to it.

Getting a grip on Adversity
is best when we catch it early on.
When out of foresight, anticipation, preparation, and
readiness, we see it coming,
and being prepared for it,
we prevent it or stop it right in its tracks,
before it happens,
right at its onset.

And yet,
in many ways Adversity is also an opportunity,
sometimes for renewal, new beginnings,
or simply, marking the start of the end of a bad spell.

How we react and cope with it,
determines our success
in overcoming and making something positive out of it.

If hardship is <u>avoidable</u>, then our existential duty
is to do all within our power,
to prevent it or stay out of its path.

But, on the other hand, if adversity is <u>inevitable</u>,
we must adapt or learn to live with it,
as our goal is to outlast and outwill it.

If hardship is <u>irreversible</u>,
we will still seek to find and squeeze the most out of life,
during every moment we are in the Universe.

On the other hand,
if hardship is <u>mendable</u>,
we fight like lions,
to cure ourselves,
doing it relentlessly to no end.

Yet, we must be very careful of mirages in the desert,
as hardships sometimes
are nothing but a figment of our imagination,
where we see obstacles and hurdles
where there are none.

We create them out of fear, insecurities,
pessimism, anxiety, or even depressive conditions.

Adversity is best faced with existential tools
like hope, conviction, resilience, defiance,
optimism, ingenuity, faith, work ethic,
a busy mind, and a spirit with a purpose,
all of these coupled with love.

Sometimes we run into the Adversity of others,
don't know what to do,
involuntarily our perception of them becomes negative
as if those afflicted with Adversity,
suffer from a very contagious disease,
we want to stay away from.

On other occasions,
we act as if, in a way,
those under hardship have somehow suddenly changed
or fallen from their former selves,
so, we perceive them and behave as if,
because of their circumstances,
they are less,
hence not worthy of us.

But how wrong we are
to conduct ourselves in such ways,
as inexorably we'll end up
experiencing hardship and tragedy as well,
finding ourselves on the receiver's end
of the same exact happenstance.

Thus, it is wise and existential
to treat the hardship of others,
with utmost respect, and a kind-giving heart,
as even if their battles are not ours,
remember,
we are still soldiers of the same army,
fighting the same existential war.

Against unforeseen mishaps and vicissitudes,
hardship is greatly diminished when thought of
in comparative and relative terms,
as no matter how difficult and bad the circumstances may seem,
they can always be a lot worse.

Adversity is at its worst when it comes unannounced,
we are unprepared,
and are caught unguarded.

The best of all attitudes against Adversity
is to treat it as an enemy of war,
to whom we never surrender,
against whom we never quit,
to the contrary, we fight and oppose relentlessly,
until we defeat, or do away with it.

But if we can't, we adapt,
continuing to extract out of Adversity,
the best life still has to offer
within the circumstances that we face,
knowing there is never time to waste,
because life never stops,
while we overcome hardship.

Finally,
Adversity must always be treated
as an existential opportunity to wake up
from a life of contentment, comfort, and complacency.
Hence, hardship can be a chance to renew, and reinvent ourselves.
But, Adversity is an opportunity only if we make it so.

"How Is It That You Make Me Feel So Special?"

What are all those little things you do?
What is it about the way you act?
What are those spell binding words you say?
What is it about all those magical verses you scribble?

All of it, makes me feel so special, my love.

Is it that you make me feel whimsical,
happy, loved, adored,
and revered to no end?

Or is it?
That I am reminded everyday
with the whirlwind of all of it,
that I am
the most important person in the world to you,
and the center of your Universe.

This is the only way I can explain, how,
while basking in joy,
I have no choice but to feel
motivated, inspired, and grateful.

That's how,
you bring out the best in me,
and the most I can give,
just because the way you are,
and how you make me feel,
so special,
so unique,
my love.

"Coherence"
(Figuring Things Out in Life)

Figuring things out in life is to clearly define,
What we want out of life?
What we have a propensity for?
How we like to live?
Who we chose to be with?
What we believe in?
What we strive to accomplish?
What we intend to leave as our legacy?

Because, in the end,
we must seek and figure out,
what life means to us.
Otherwise,
we'll wander through it with lifeless souls and empty spirits.

Figuring out life's meaning,
allows us to decipher, determine,
what our purpose and direction are.

Otherwise,
we'll bounce and sail through it
like a rudderless vessel,
or a craft without compass.

Life's formula is different for each one of us,
the recipe of "how to live"
is unique for each individual.
What makes sense for one, few or many,
may not make sense to others at all.

Thus, to avoid living someone else's life
by copying their "sense making,"
we have to figure out first,
what works for us in life,
and then, what works for others.

In order to figure things out in life,
we need Coherence,
the glue that connects it all together.

Coherence is connecting in "sensical-harmony"

Our life with our aspirations and beliefs,

Our actions with our dreams and goals,

Our line of work, vocation, art or craft
with our best talents, and abilities,

Our passions with mundane life,

Our convictions, and ideals
with what we practice in our daily lives,

Our values and virtues with our faith,

Out tempo with our life's clock,

Our awareness of every second we have left on planet earth,

Our family, loved ones, fellow human beings,
and the objects of our desire
with our feelings,
and the best side of our essence and nature.

Making sense and figuring things out in life
is to coherently connect
our life's meaning with our life's purpose.

"Virtue"

Just by arriving on planet earth and being alive,
we are born in grace,
but we are not born in virtue.

Virtue has to be acquired over time
through hard work and perseverance.

Virtues are not obsequious,
to the contrary,
they have to be learned and applied,
sought and sweated,
identified and pursued,
nurtured and harvested,
cultivated with discipline,
and developed with sacrifice.

We acquire knowledge
seeking to learn insight, wisdom, and good judgment.

We build brave hearts and fortitude
to build and develop courage, tenacity, and valor.

We practice compassion and benevolence
in order to learn how to empathize and be mindful,
and perennially in love with mankind.

We exercise unwavering truthfulness, and unflinching integrity
to cement our honesty, honor, probity, and good name.

We exercise serenity and silence
in order to be paused, considerate, and thoughtful.

We live in order and neatness
to become structured, methodical, and organized.

We pursue righteousness and rightfulness
in order to achieve fairness, correctness, and impartiality.

We exhibit "unflickering" hope, boundless generosity,
endless gratitude, and genuine humility
aiming to exceed and surpass
all we've received while forming our legacy out of it.

As our virtues grow,
they mature into a condition of noble excellence.

As they develop,
our virtues become the genesis and the enablers
of our beliefs and value system.

Virtues are imperative tools of life,
without chasing, and procuring them,
we are not fully functional,
or coherent as human beings,
as we would be marching through life with blinders on,
unable to extract the fruits of joy
from a life in full.

Our virtues are the foundation of our values,
which in turn are the pillars of our character,
hence, without a solid set of virtues,
our values will be incomplete or flawed,
causing seismic faults in our character.

Being virtuous is to be equipped
with a precious set of attributes of excellence
to conduct ourselves in life
under extraordinary standards
of nobility, righteousness, sensibility, and rightfulness
under the mantel of inspiration and joy,
from a life in virtue,
a "Life in Full."

"Forgiveness"

What is it to forgive?
Is it to erase from our memory
those feelings of fused anger and hurt,
lingering resentments, or existential wounds,
caused either by the acts of others, or life vicissitudes?

Or is it to pardon transgressions, or betrayals by those we trust?

Or is it to absolve disloyalty from those we count on?

Or is it to excuse the consequential untruths
coming from those we blindly believe in?

Or is it to acquit the irreplaceable losses created by those we rely on?

Or is it to send into remission the offenses
to our decency, dignity, honor, and self-respect,
perpetuated by those we follow?

Or is it to actually forgive ourselves first?

However, the problem with forgiving our own acts,
is that we seek pardon from others first,
as if looking to assuage our guilt,
through the absolution imparted to us
by the words and gestures of others.

Guilt cannot be fooled by fantasies or falsehoods,
the feeling of culpability dissolves,
only when our conscience says and allows us to do so.

Because,
where forgiveness truly happens first,
is within ourselves.
Only through a genuine acceptance of responsibility
are all our feelings of guilt absconded, and go away...

This is how the stern watch of our conscience is appeased,
opening the doors for us to be absolved.

Then and only then, what others think or say,
brings completeness to forgiveness' virtuous circle,
one built out of authenticity, and truthfulness.

Once inside this loop,
we can finally reach atonement.

When do we sincerely forgive?
Sometimes we pretend to forgive,
but we really don't, denying its actuality.

Sometimes we are simply unwilling to do so.
Both attitudes are poisonous to the spirit,
and destructive to the soul,
because the longer they linger,
the more our true selves erode,
the deeper our sadness becomes
and the more devastating the damage is
to our ability to live a life in full.

To truly forgive,
we must be genuinely willing and disposed
to have the courage to face and look
at the pain, the wound, the offenses, or their personas
straight in the eye, confronting them.

Then whatever or whoever is afflicting us,
we must let go
at whatever pace our heart allows us.

But regardless of anything of anyone,
we must always seek finality and closure
in order to reach atonement.

What does it take to forgive?
How do we know we have in fact forgiven?

We know it because our ability to forgive
is a requirement for our personal growth,
as well as the enrichment and evolution of our entire self.

Without the capacity to forgive,
our virtues and values have flaws,
and our meaning and purpose in life,
while preoccupied with overcoming the haze,
are clouded and murky.

And without forgiveness we are stuck in reverse,
without oxygen or inspiration
to breath and infuse life into our spirit and soul.

Forgiveness is also a precondition to experience the joy of living.
Because without it,
happiness is hampered, limited, and handicapped.

<u>The genesis of the noble virtue of forgiveness
is the magical elixir of compassion and piety</u>:
As with compassion we connect and empathize
with the pain and sorrow of those in need of atonement,
as with piety we are illuminated and enlightened by grace,
enabling us to devote ourselves,
with dutiful respect, sincerity, and veneration
to the atonement of ours and others' faults.

When we forgive,
We throw a mantel of goodness
on everyone and everything around us.

When we forgive,
our life renews itself,
and our existential time machine's hands
move in the right direction.

When we forgive,
a torrent of lava, right from our very own center of the earth,
explodes into the sky,
freeing our core, our essence,
from life's heaviest
emotional anchors, ballasts, or dead weights.

When we forgive,
we become worthier,
thus, more likely, to be rewarded
with forgiveness as well.

When we forgive,
we elevate ourselves to a state
of compassionate and pious grace,
where we can seek atonement
for our spirit and soul.

"Silence Within The Music"

There's stillness in the air,
no sound within the music,
fidelity exclaims perfection.

The notes sing glory,
there is purity in the air,
the violins weep,
the cellos cry,
the trumpets sing,
the piano chants
to the deepest ends of our hearts.

There is perfection in the room,
absolute serenity in harmony,
flawless stillness with room to spare
to meditate and wander
to no end.

There is silence within the music,
there is silence as it plays,
there is silence in the air.

"Reciprocity"

As water drops,
Nature blossoms.

As the sun shines,
all the colors of the world light up around us.

As night falls,
the entire Universe high up in the sky glows.

As we breath,
our entire self
gets to live another day.

As we are able to see,
reality's images come to life for us to enjoy.

As we think,
out entire world exists.

The worlds of physics and
biology can be calculated,
measured,
and in part explained,
through reciprocity.
Part of the essence of life's virtuous cycle
is reciprocity.

If constant motion
is the roar of nature's engine at work,
reciprocity is the key component
of the fuel that enables it.

When we reciprocate with each other,
we appeal to the better angels
dwelling in ourselves, and over humanity.

The true essence of receiving anything in life
lies in what we've given beforehand.

In a way,
we have not truly given anything,
if nothing comes back.

Inexorably, sooner or later,
if we do good things and we do them right,
if we perform good deeds,
life will respond by giving back to us in spades.

But if we don't,
one way or another,
life will get back at us,
in the most unexpected of fashions,
and everything and anything
we've taken or received,
without reciprocity in return,
will be taken back,
confiscated,
even yanked from us.

If we shoot arrows and bullets or throw stones,
we should expect them to rebound at some point,
perhaps with even more impact in return.

If we gift, dote good deeds, books, and roses,
they'll come back in troves.

Mutuality is an immutable correlation of greater than one,
never, a one-way street.

Generosity is intrinsic to reciprocity and vice-versa.

Their joint power creates endless virtuous circles,
positive, and upward spirals
of never ending gives and takes.

To reciprocate is to be eternally grateful,
to life, humankind, and The Creator,
in a way is about
paying forward to others as well,
for the privilege of being alive.

All of it,
with the lingering, and handsome reward
that all we've contributed to life itself and others,
perhaps more,
will be paid back to us in spades.

"Defiance"

When it happens for legitimate, and valid reasons,
defiance is a deliberate and positive attitude,
an existential tool that helps us
challenge and confront any kind of hardship.

It's such an indomitable force
that regardless of life's obstacles,
unbearable circumstances,
material or emotional shortcomings,
even profound pain and sorrow,
once experienced,
unleashed,
and through it,
neither our resilience,
our will or our desire to live,
much less our fighting spirit,
can ever be bent or tamed.

When we resist,
in the name of truth,
defending freedom, dignity, and justice,

When we oppose
oppression, persecution, and tyranny,

When we antagonize
bigotry, hate and, discrimination,

When we stand immutable
behind virtue, values, and principle,

Defiance becomes *intrinsical*
to what drives and sustains us,
to how we withstand and outlast it all,
and to how in the end, we prevail.

Defiance is the purest expression,
and release valve of our inner raging fires,
those that lie right at our core,
those that can never be put away
as they burn and churn,
fueling our deepest passions,
our most unshakeable convictions,
and our firmest beliefs.

Defiance is our fiercest and most animalistic display
of the sheer force of utter will and steely resolve,
against anything or anyone,
difficult and unsavory as it maybe,
that life could throws at us.

Defiance is the attitude that defines us best,
as true "life warriors,"
those that not only,
can't be conquered by hardship,
but to the contrary, face it square in the eye,
attacking it relentlessly,
treating it as an enemy of war,
going at it until it is totally
vanquished, obliterated, and defeated.

Defiance is an existential weapon
we carry with us at all times,
to bend and break hardship's aim and will.

d

In defiance is how we turn the tables around
to face life's vicissitudes.

It is how we drown, conquer, and defeat our fears,
as well as defeat
some of life's greatest impostors.

"Curiosity"

When we itch to explore,
When we crave to adventure,
When we have an inkling to discover,
When we can't wait to incessantly
dig, search, find, check, investigate,
analyze, study, experiment, and validate incessantly,

When we are not afraid of change,
the unknown, unseen, anyone, or anything new,

When we are,
keen to break the mold,
swim against the stream,
oblivious to conventional wisdom,
and able to improvise or adapt
in the spur of the moment,

When we can contemplate life
with candid, innocent, and dreamy hearts,

When we are not intimidated by,
How High, How Deep, How Low,
How Big, How Small, How Impactful,
How Irrelevant, How Celebrated,
How Despised, How Demanding,
How Patient, How Calm,
How Passionate, How Disheartened,
How Defeated, How Triumphant,
we may be, go, or become,

Then,
We are in possession
of the magic elixir of Curiosity,
a whimsical existential-inducing bug,

that places us,
on a riveting journey,
where we float above mundane reality,
under the mantle of an endless pursuit
to be awed, amazed, or simply blown away
by the acquisition of precious
knowledge, and experience.

Curiosity takes us,
to countless labyrinths, mystical places,
memorable people, and transcendental moments.

Curiosity engages and dotes on us restless spirits,
as well as,
a soul soaked with "the light and energy of life."

As an agent of change in the pursuit of wisdom,
curiosity is one of the most valuable
existential tools there is.

Through curiosity,
we constantly refine our life's purpose
by revisiting, renewing, and defining
our life's meaning.

With Curiosity,
we remain goofy, loose, joyful, and foolish:
endlessly looking, searching, learning, and discovering
someone, something, anything...! Anew.

If we deploy and employ curiosity,
we are always ready for "change,"
hence,
we easily embrace evolution as well.

"Decisions"

There is no worst decision in life
than the one we never make,
which is not to be confused
with deciding to do nothing
or take no action
as those are still decisions
we would've made.

Why is it?
That, there are so many of us
so utterly indecisive
that we are simply
unable to take decisions
on or about lives,
ourselves,
or our future.

Decisions to ponder, wander and wonder.
Decisions we nail, or blunder,
contest or tender,
waste or reap,
reach or press,
accept or reject,
rejoice or despise,
elevate or bury,
doubt or believe in,
pursue or avoid,
reverse or affirm,
lament or relish,
reluctantly take,
or passionately embrace.

Decisions, decisions, decisions to make
about which paths to follow,
the alternatives we choose
or the course of action to pick.

Being decisive is hard and difficult
as it requires us to conquer
our worst insecurities and fears.

Decisiveness is a consequence
of resoluteness and determination
to bring matters to a conclusion,
one way or another.

Being decisional is the result of our readiness
to form actionable options
and to act on them,
through the selection
of the available choices we face.

Decisions always reap guidance.

Through decisions
is how the dynamics of life takes place,
and it is how everyone and everything,
for better or worse,
forwards and backwards,
moves and responds
in the circle of life.

In this context,
to decide is not a choice,
but an existential imperative,
as without it,
we fall into a catatonic void
and our life takes place without us,
passing us by.

Decisions, decisions, decisions to make.
Decisions that overwhelm and suck the air out of us.
Decisions that keep coming,
and never go away.

To be alive involves decisionism,
There is no way around it.

Thus, when a choice presents itself,
to form an opinion,
make a choice
or choose a path to act and follow,
take the decision,
and move on.

Decisions are imminent choices,
we permanently must face,
as long as we are participants
in the circle of life.

"Resilience"

Resilience lies at the core
of the very essence of the human spirit.

It's a vital and virtuous existential condition,
comprised of sheer strength of character
and awesome, utter willfulness.

Resilience is
the untamable drive,
burning fire,
unflinching defiance,
relentless resistance,
fearless courage,
stubborn perseverance,
unwavering belief,
and unstoppable hunger,
required to live
with the intensity, passion, and endurance
needed to succeed at any endeavor.

The resilient person,
tries again,
never stops,
does not give in to exhaustion,
bounces back,
moves forward,
does not dwell on the past,
adapts in an instant,
perennially studies,
learns,
and ignores rejection.

The resilient person,
uses fear as a strength,
and does not comprehend the words,

boredom,
gossip,
lingering grudges,
or jealousy.

The resilient person
endures hardship,
overcomes tragedy,
learns from criticism,
treats failure as an opportunity,
mistakes as lessons,
defeats as temporary,
uses "noes" as incentives,
and never, ever quits,
much less surrenders.

Resilience is that quasi "super-human force"
that allows us,
to embark on challenging and demanding quests,
with strength and self-confidence,
to endure right up to completion and beyond,
despite seemingly insurmountable challenges,
setbacks, and difficulties,
to dare life,
defying all odds,
with the absolute conviction and self-belief,
that no matter who or what, how, when, or where,
we will in the end,
succeed.

"Life, Beauty And Art"

Where does beauty reside?
Where does it lie?
Where is it found?

Beauty begins with us,
inside all of us,
ready to be discovered,
ready to be tapped.

In order for us to see beauty
in anyone or anything,
we must see and recognize it first,
within ourselves.

Where else can beauty be found?
Well, by understanding that starts within,
we can realize and appreciate
that we are surrounded by it as well.

The beauty we possess is what enables us
to find it in everyone and everything else.

However, more often than not,
attractiveness is not always apparent at first sight.

Because there is,
dirt and darkness where diamonds are hidden.

Mud and disease where gold can be found,
seemingly buried behind impenetrable rocks or sands.

There is,
Litter and Chaos
where masterpieces are born,

Debris and Dust
where magnificent craftsmanship takes place,

Slime and Sulfur
where oil riches burst forth,

Incoherence and Lack of Meaning
in the words and statements
found within the finest scribbles
when they are first created,

And Pain, Sweat and Tears
when he noblest human feats come to pass.

Where does beauty originate?
Sometimes beauty is born in ugliness.
Beauty is best valued,
when uncovered from underneath,
or within hideousness.

Beauty is best appreciated
when provided or defined
under a mantle
that runs contrary
to stereotype and conventional wisdom.

Beauty is also conferred in spades
and rich bounties to many,
who in turn fail to recognize
its existential worthiness,
and therefore,
fail to enjoy the aesthetics of life's
most magnificent, radiant, and incandescent side.

When beauty does not provide intense satisfaction,
to our spirit and soul,
it may be passing,
empty and hollow.

In all its dimensions,
beauty,
whether in persons or possessions,
over the passage of time
requires our benevolent disposition
to be recognized and admired.
Beauty changes and morphs
as life's clock ticks,
but in the eyes of those
that truly know how to enjoy and feel it,
beauty never fades, diminishes, or goes away.

Physical youth provides and masks beauty for all of us, but through the years,
the beauty and richness, or lack of,
of our life, spirit, and soul,
are progressively plastered
and reflected on our faces
in such ways, that inevitably,
we end up revealing and exposing
what and who we really are inside, without a mask.

Life's truest beauty lies in hiding
ready to be uncovered,
if we make the effort to do so.

The beauty of a life well lived,
ages with nobility and grace.

Beauty is to be found in those life travelers,
that live free of limiting dogmas,
prejudices or stereotypes.
Those that truly find and enjoy
pulchritude, attractiveness,
liveliness, comeliness, charm, grace
and anyone or anything pleasing to the senses.
Those that truly celebrate all aspects of life,
Those that truly love and are loved,
Those that give without truly expecting anything in return
Those that are active participants in their lives,

Those that dispense and value
the small gestures and details in life.
Those that devote, pour their hearts and spirits
into everything they do,
and live passionate, inspired and happy lives.
Those are the ones possessing,
and appreciative of lasting beauty.
The kind of beauty that regardless
of what our senses prompt us to do,
regardless of place or circumstances,
regardless of age or riches,
regardless of ourselves or others,
never goes away.

Lasting beauty is perhaps
one of the most precious existential gifts,
and perhaps one of the hardest to master.

It requires development as an immanent quality or virtue,
to appreciate, wear, value, and treasure beauty,
even if there isn't any
to be obviously seen, perceived, or found.

But, when does Beauty becomes art?
Art is inherent to Beauty
as Beauty is to art.
Art is born in Beauty.
Art creates Beauty.

Beauty must be perceived and acknowledged,
for Art to exist.

As Art transforms the ordinary into masterful
and the extraordinary into sublime,
Art alters our perception,
making the object not only appealing,
but also arising feelings
that have meaning and purpose to us.

Art creates an intimate, quasi-spiritual,
and highly intense connection within us,
because it speaks the language of our spirit
and is a mirror to our soul.

Art resonates to beauty
as it always infatuates our hearts,
as beauty is always driven and born out of it.

As Beauty,
Art only exists in the eye of the beholder,
but if it does,
then, there are no limits or boundaries
to what can be Art,
it can be a scribble, an essay, any craft.
Inexorably, anything Beauty touches,
may easily translate into Art.

Art is a deliberate human creation driven
by inspiration, talent, skill,
and specially our hearts.

Art, even unintentionally,
always is generated
through bursting emotions,
then tempered and polished
through method, technique, and intuitive studies
in the realms of knowledge and intellect.

Art is grace and blessing
as one can't help
but to feel the hand of God
behind its masterfulness and Beauty.

At the crossroads between Beauty and Art,
resides the most sublime of connections
between the human spirit, soul
and everything we create.

Art is where life's mastery lies,
where all our best and unique talents are harvested,
where continuous inspiration and happiness effervesce.

When we master Art and Beauty,
we are truly and genuinely alive,
as both require our vital engagement.
A heightened sensorial state,
where connected with Creation,
we become champions of life
by squeezing and enjoying
some of the best it has to offer.

"What An Amazing Day This Is!"

What an amazing day this is!
Today, I woke up on the surface of Mars
surrounded by a landscape of rocks and sand
with intense shades of red and rusty dust
that soon became monotonous
with the look of spiritless butterscotch caramel.

There's not air to breath here
as the atmosphere is 95% CO_2.
There's hardly any water either,
as whatever there is
lies underneath its poles,
thus, certainly not within my reach.

Nothing grows here either.
There's no life of any kind.
It's a dead planet.

And as I turn and gaze up at the night sky,
I see the resplendence of the Earth in the distance,
and it immediately seizes me.

Our planet splendor glows,
Its light beams life
into every direction of the Universe.
Its greens, blues and whites
touch me deep, deep inside,
and their beauty and richness
provoke this fierce sense of belonging
that simply bursts out and overwhelms me.

"That's my home," I declare.
"That's where I live," I point to the sky.

Then, as I look at my surroundings,
my living planet's presence stands out
in stark contrast to the dead red planet
I am standing on.

At that moment, I realize
that the gallery of asteroids, comets, meteors,
moons, planets, and stars in the firmament,
to the best of my knowledge,
are also dead.

Seemingly, our planet is,
as a biological entity, the only one alive!

Today,
I woke up on the surface of Mars
and felt both,
undeservingly privileged and eternally grateful
for being alive to enjoy
such an amazing place like our awesome planet.

Today,
I woke up inside a 10-nanometer chip,
packing 100 million transistors,
capable of processing algorithmic calculations,
and software so powerful
that eventually will make
every product and service be so smart,
that they'll emulate the human brain.

Today,
I woke up in a world where we, humans,
are enhancing every day
what Nature and God have provided us,
achieving unimaginable
levels of progress and development.

And I am alive right in the middle of it as it's happening,
giving me the opportunity to take advantage of,
and enjoy the benefits
these quantum leaps of progress bring,
Who can ask for better fortune!

Today,
I woke up inside of me,
and the first thing I did,
was travel at the speed of light
through the wirings of my brain.
And in the end, navigating all of my grey matter,
was a distance equivalent to the circumference of the earth.

Next, with the most powerful computer in existence,
I decided to count the number of cells giving me life:
First, I tallied the number of neurons in my brain
and came up with several billion.

Then, I wanted to see
how all of the rest of the cells in my body work,
and soon after, I found myself
filling screen after screen with of billions of them as well.
Each cell was independent
and fulfilled different missions,
but all perfectly co-existing organically amongst each other.

Then, I was shocked to witness tens of thousands
of the same vital cells dying
just to be simultaneously replaced
by new ones reproduced at the same instant.

Not yet satisfied,
my curiosity let me to witness firsthand,
how viruses and infections continuously swarm my body,
and how many thousands upon thousands
of sick cells or pathogens inhabitant me at any given moment
ready to conduct a sneak attack.

Again, I was startled to learn that I am,
like the rest of us,
infested with bacteria,
which turns out stimulates immune systems,
so is vital for any kind of life to exist.

And yet,

I was able to watch how my defense mechanisms keep
every threat under control
by either eradicating
or simply keeping it at bay.

Finally, I was able to inspect all of my organs while at work.
I marveled at their inexorability and vitality,
as well as their beauty and perfection,
as they endlessly perform highly complex tasks with ease.

Today,
I woke inside of me and realized
that just the mere fact of being alive is a continuous miracle
that renews itself each and every second.

Today,
I finally understood that
being alive is a delicate balance,
that there is a very fine line
between, death, sickness, and health.

Today,
I woke inside of me and was able to see
how infinitely complex my whole self is,
and how
in order to be here on Earth,
I've been provided
with this amazing organism
—my body—
And that is how I finally understood
how precious every moment is.

Today,
I woke up on the top of the world,
and felt the air flow through my lungs
while realizing that just a couple of minutes
without it, and that's it, Life is Gone!

Then I observed, and learned
What are the food, and weather cycles,
and the human nutrients needed to be grown,
harvested, and produced to feed us.

Then, I realized.
How a little time it would take for us
to weaken and even starve
if it wasn't for the abundance that surrounds us.

Then, I saw billions of fellow human beings all around me,
and realized that our planet and nature as a whole
provide for all of us, with equal perfection,
all our basic subsistent needs,
as if we are a single cell organism.

Today,
I woke up and realized,
that live on the only known "living" planet in the Universe.

Today,
I woke and finally understood
how very, very few of us
make it from reproductive cells into human beings.

Today,
I finally woke up, to life.
Today,
I finally feel truly alive.
Today,
Once and for all
I feel grateful for simply being alive.

What an Amazing day this is!
What an amazing life,
and what an amazing pair of vessels,
my planet, and my body,
I've been provided with.

So,
What am I waiting for?
What are You waiting for?
What are We waiting for?

Let's go out and enjoy that we are ALIVE!

"Serenity, Courage and Wisdom"

Serenity is a contemplative state
of absolute inner peace,
and deliberate, immutable calmness.

It's a condition of placidness
that allows us to observe life's movie from the outside.

In slow motion,
we seemingly pause and contemplate each single frame,
and the false perception
of time flying or dragging its feet
simply disappears,
giving way to a refreshing, genuine measure of time.
Serenity is also a key ingredient to moderation,
whether on a meditative, pensive,
reflective or contemplative mode.

Calmness and placidness
are conduits and facilitators
to caution, refrain, restrain, tolerance and prudence,
while being at the same time,
the best antidotes against reactive and impulsive behavior.

By fostering modicum in our conduct,
serenity enables us to have
the ability to contemplate our alternatives and options
while taking enough time to make decisions.

Do we choose serene inaction
or
Do we decide to act with our gut, brains, heart,
or a combination of them?

In Serenity life slows down,
our frantic pace freezes,
and we find peace in pause.
But perhaps serenity's greatest virtue
is acceptance or acknowledgment

of inevitable, irreplaceable, or irreversible realities.
Hence, Serenity is one of our best
existential weapons against denial.

And by providing us with clarity and finality, even closure,
serenity becomes a key ingredient of courage.

The more bravery and valor are impregnated with serenity,
the fiercer, and more invincible, they are.

In the absence of serenity,
courage may be nothing more than a suicide mission.

Courage is our best resource
for overcoming extreme adversity and hardship,
seemingly insurmountable obstacles and difficulties,
devastation, and total defeat,
loss or failure, and overwhelming odds against.

Courage is also our best weapon
to tame and conquer our fears.

And that is how,
when acting with bravery and valor
fear becomes our ally,
instead of a paralyzing excuse.

Fearlessness is an "intrinsical" part
of the fuel driving courage's fire...

Thus,
Fearlessness becomes the reason to act,
in order to prevent or reverse
the consequences of what we are afraid of.

That's how courage is flushed with positive and actionable fear.

When in action as we execute,
courage is fearless, dauntless, and intrepid.

As it relates to courage and serenity,
wisdom provides us
with enlightenment, sagacity,
and judicious behavior
to decide either
for <u>Serenity</u>
to be able to accept crude realities,
and to defeat denial
or for <u>Courage</u>
to allow us to reverse
the improbable, the impossible, the irreversible,
and the seemingly inevitable,
or to use <u>both of them</u>
according to the circumstances.

"The Fable of The Old Young Man and The Jester"

The joker walks back
heading towards to his "Camerino,"
as the crowd at the circus main tent stage
still cheers his act.

He has a white plastered face
with a perpetual smile,
a giant painted mouth
a tiny perfectly round nose,
both painted in red.

He wears a tall, floppy
multicolored hat,
covering shoulder length
bright orange strands of hair.

His loose clothes
on one side
resemble those of a harlequin
and have polka dots of white
on the other.

His humongous shoes
seem to like two flapping tongues,
impossible wide at the front,
unbelievable narrow at the back.

His nonchalant antics
so often are shocking and outrageous
as everyone and everything
are subjects of his jest,
as all of his actions
seem like a parody of reality,
a mime's journey
into the lighter side of life.

But not all is as it appears to be
in our existence
or is it?

The diminutive voce interrupts his stride
"Jester, jester!"
Pleads de young juvenile in the alley.

The clown turns and stares at the young teenager
with his penetrating green eyes.

"Isn't it a bit too far off the beaten path
for a young man like you
to be wandering around?"
The impatient clown asks.

"My parents are just behind the curtains
feeding the giraffes with my little brother,
they know I am here,"
the young man replies with confidence.

"Fair enough,"
Says the clown in resignation.

Pensively the youngster crosses both arms
while raising one hand to his chin.

"Joker, do you make people laugh for a living?"
the young man asks in all seriousness.

"Isn't causing laughter what clowns do?"
The clown replies in the form of a riddle.

Unfazed, the young man quizzes him further.
"You make people happy Jester.
Are you a happiness maker then?"

The clown relaxes
as he leans over the door of his camerino.

"After all, isn't that
what those that come to the circus seek?"
The clown replies yet with another question,
while still giving close to nothing to his young admirer.

"Now, if you can excuse me,"
the clown says as he steps into his dressing room.

"Joker, joker," the young man pleads,
and presses forward before the door closes.
The startled clown pauses.

"I don't find you very funny in person, Sir!
Your face wears a painted smile but up close,
it doesn't feel genuine,
because your eyes exude sadness,
and specially anger, perhaps at me,"
the young man blurts out on impulse.

The clown's first reaction is to pull away,
but to his great surprise,
he hesitates and reverses himself.

"You're a very good observer, little man.
Come over and have a seat,"
the jester offers unexpectedly.

Instinctively,
the clown leaves the door wide open.

Once seated, he offers the young man,
a box full of chocolates,
letting him pick up whichever he wants.

"Joker, you make others happy, but not yourself, why?"
The young man asks.

"Isn't it, by the way, how many live,
just keeping appearances in public,

but guarding their darker inner realities
close to their vests?"
Replies the joker, once more, with another question.

"Jester, when I looked at you from afar,
while doing what you love and do best,
making others laugh,
being lauded for by everyone,
for an instant,
your life seemed like a fairy tale,
but now being next to you,
I ask myself,
how is it that you are not happy?"
The opinionated young man asks while puzzled.

"Inquisitive youngster, isn't it true that in life,
there's always something missing
that which we covet the most,
but we don't have it, nor can we reach it?"
The jester reasons.

"Or is it that we are always on the way,
chasing goals,
and when we finally reach them,
the goal posts already moved,
most of the time by us
and a new pursuit has replaced it all?"
states the jester in full sarcasm.

"Joker, but what you have at present is enough, isn't it?
what is often called "the chase,"
is filled with life mementos,
and those that love what you do
are all there to enjoy your act.
You have to celebrate
the journey of life as it happens, otherwise,
you're missing most of it,"
the youngster declares in wisdom.

"There are no fairy tales in life kid,
those only reside in children's books,
and in the world of fantasy,"
Once more, the clown counters back in contempt.

"My life is a fairy tale, Jester"
the young man states in joy.

"I'm sure it is,
You're surely born in a privileged home,
enjoying all the trappings of wealth and success.
Happily married parents,
no hardship, no tragedy, no pain.
Of course, you see life as a fairy tale,
but be ready though, the moment will come,
when you won't see it that way anymore,"
states the clown with poignant criticism.

"Joker, I'm an orphan,
those are my adoptive parents,
we were homeless until recently
as my father just got a job as a janitor.
My youngest brother walks with crutches
because he contracted polio when he was five,"
declares the young man with words filled with deep emotions.

The clown covers his mouth in shock and shame.
"I'm so, so..." he starts to apologize,
only to be interrupted by the youngster.

"Jester, you're a privileged man.
Take stock of all you have going for yourself
and turn it into your source of joy.
Use your daily access to happiness and laughter,
for what they are, celebrations of life.
You fairy tale in life resides in you.
You do what you love, people love what you do,
is there more to ask out of life?

Fact is, that if you wished to, you could make
out of any circumstance, place, and people around you,
participants in your life's fairy tales,"
the young man declares with profound wisdom.

"I understand now the source of wisdom,
way beyond your years, in your words,"
the clown declares.

"And what would that be, Sir?"
The young man quizzes.

"Hardship is what made you who you are,"
the jester states.

"Life is a fairy tale
that resides inside all of us.
It is there to be tapped,
regardless of place or circumstances.
It only requires
ingenuity and candor of the soul,
and a true desire of the spirit
to live throughout the journey of life,"
are the youngster's parting words.

His parents and brother approach through the corridor.
"Time to go,"
they announce.
The young man walks out with a big broad smile.
"Joker, it was very kind of you to spend time with me,
it was a truly magical moment,"
he declares, his face radiating joy.

"Young man,
it was magical for me as well; it was like a..."
he says in surprise
while stopping short,
filled with emotion...

"A fairy tale?"
The young man asks smiling even more.

"It most definitely was,
and a life lesson well learned too,"
says the clown with sparkling eyes
that finally make for once,
his face painted smile, real and genuine,
perhaps forever.

"A Very Particular Symbiosis"

I am all of you, You are all of me.

We are all of you, We are all of me.

You are me. I am you.

We are,
only one of you,
only one of me.

Only one of us,
one and only,
you and I,
both of us,
forever.

"The case of The curious child and The Restless Magician"

He wears a blue cap filled with silver stars
overlooking an electric blue coat.
His top hat is slightly tilted to the right,
and his magic wand is black with silver tips.

Over a bit more than an hour's passing,
he's defied gravity,
and all of the senses of his patrons.
He's read minds,
cut some in half,
made others disappear,
done the unexpected,
and made everyone exclaim
in awe and amazement at his acts.

It all climaxes on a grand finale
where he floats in the air,
and suddenly disappears
amidst a controlled explosion of fireworks
sparkling all around him.
He soon reappears high up,
just to disappear on the balconies
only to pop again at the main stage
to wave and thank the ecstatic crowd.

As the magician ends his illusionary act
and walks hurriedly offstage,
the waiting child has a million questions.

"Is it magic or fantasy?"
Asks the curious child.

"It is both,"
answers the restless magician.

"If it is one, then it cannot be the other,"
insists the inquisitive boy.

"Why?"
Replies the impatient sorcerer.

"Because it's either real or not,"
continues the little one.

"Magic and fantasy are one and the same,"
explains the illusionist.

"Then neither is real,"
the youngster promptly concludes.

"For some yes, but for others, both are real,
and it all resides in the eye of the beholder,"
clarifies the magician.

"But how can a fantasy be real?"
asks the now obfuscated inquisitor.

"If it is real to you then that's your reality,
that is the sign of a restless spirit,
one that lives in its own reality,"
states the wise illusionist
while he pulls a little paper from his hat.

"This old scribble defines it best,
it is called -The Restless Spirit-"
The magician starts to read in earnest...

The restless spirit possesses
an itch to live,
an urge to seek,
a need to explore,
an imperative to search.

The restless soul
makes a choice of what to pursue.

The bug of restlessness,
the root of such itchiness,
that keeps our life engines,
incessantly active,
is curiosity.

Curiosity is a condition of spontaneous inquisitiveness,
a gut driven eagerness,
to learn, and to explore new things.

Curiosity and restlessness are human attitudes.
that inexorably lead
to the creation of ideas
about things that yet don't exist.

The totality of civilization and human progress
is derived from ideas,
that at first were to others,
just fantasies within their imagination,
but they were very real
to the dreamers themselves.

Magic and fantasy are both the same type of reality,
but one we have to dream out first.

But these types of dreamers are uncommon,
as they all possess restless and curious spirits,
filled with magic and fantasy,
both deliberately distorted realities,
just waiting to be made."

"Thank You, Mr. Illusionist, Thank You so much,"
says the child with his head filled
with curiosity, restlessness
along with a touch of magic, and fantasy as well.

"By The Hand of The Scribbler"

Through the hand of the scribbler
his spirit and soul burst out.

His words convey his deepest feelings,
his inspiration is spontaneous,
surging out of his serene spirit and tranquil soul.

The images and sensations take shape coming alive,
and the ideas turn into words.

As it relates to love, only the heart leads,
as the spirit and soul follow.

By the hand of the scribbler words of love come out.
They are made out of passionate fire
and boundless tenderness.

Writing to love
is easy and yet tough,
an exercise of plain contradictions.

It is so hard to find that magical inspirational moment,
but when it arrives,
all the words can be quickly, and easily written,
and their beauty shines by itself

and the verses gather strength,
all are driven in the name of love.

Through the hand of the scribbler,
his spirit and soul burst out.

And when there's love, only the heart leads,
and the spirit and soul follow.

"What An Amazing Blessing Being Together Is"

Who wrote the script of this movie?
Or is it that is made out of just our time together?
Or maybe it was us as producers and directors
of a great audience of two?

Wouldn't it be more like something predestined,
and way beyond our comprehension?
and it's always been there waiting for us,
to guide us along a wonderful path where every day,
we find more and more happiness.

A love walkway through life,
where firm ground is formed,
a safety shield
with which we can embark
on the difficult journey of life,
protected from anything that can hurt us.

A magic filter that enables us
to contemplate life,
through its better angles,
so we can extract from it,
drop by drop,
the best possible it has to offer.

A generous path that leads into many others,
seeded with goodness,
and countless flowers along the way,
that make it even prettier as we walk by.

A magic carpet upon which we live together,
taking us anywhere our imagination leads us.

This script, our script,
has been written with compressed dense ink,
that we leave behind
in this frantic ecstasy of two welded souls,
one into the other.

Two souls urged to be grateful for anything we receive,
albeit rather briefly as it soon goes away.

A script charged with the love that surrounds us.
A script's charged with strength and intensity.
A script where tenderness, passion and unconditionality
are our travel companions and the pillars of our happiness.

It is the script of the most beautiful movie ever written.
It is the script with the magnificent and predestined blessing
of you and I being together for ever.

"As To How Love Lights up Everything"

As Matter,
we are Finite,
pure and simply Dust,
and we are Ephemeral Energy,
but above all,
we are God's miracle.

As Reason,
we are Conscience,
Thoughts, and Imagination,
and in our minds,
the world is Ideas and Shadows.

As Spirit,
we are Souls in Love,
and our spirits light up life's way,
providing us with Meaning and Purpose,
and enabling us to travel far
along the Journey of Life.

Out of Matter and Reason,
only the Spirit transcends the infinite,
and the Soul is its Vital Engine.
Faith is the Light that emanates from the Soul.
The Light between all men,
originates from the Spirit,
and that is Love.

"When I write To You"

When I write to you,
I give you all of me on those little notes.

When my spirit writes to you,
I surrender perhaps, some of the best of me.

When my imagination writes about you,
I try to express in thousands of ways,
how much I love you,
and how deep my feelings are.

When my soul writes to you,
I am offering my best gifts,
those that cannot be touched,
those that can only be felt.

When my heart writes to you,
life's beauty grows,
through words,
beating like a drum that cannot be stopped,
heard by all.

When my love writes about you,
everything I feel turns into magic,
all of it yours,
without limit and to no end.

When my dreams write for you,
time, and space stop,
the words flow,
the spirit is enriched,
and the soul smiles in joy.

When my feelings write about you,
my heart is emptied out of words
that burst out,
and pour love into you.

When my joy writes about you,
there is happiness in life,
with a crystalline spirit, and an innocent soul.

Whenever I write to you in the future,
you'll know and feel that it will always be the
best, and most profound offering
that I can give and will ever give to you.

"Convergence"

Convergence and Confluence
are life's timely opportunities.

When there is convergence,
we convene and congregate
through concurrence and congruence
of common interests,
life paths come together on some form or another
out of a pre-ordained links or bonds.

Similarly,
when confluence occurs, through convocation,
we seek concertation, congeniality, and conciliation.

Convergence and Confluence
are rare and unique life opportunities.
They may be elusive, passing, and repeatable.

That's why,
when they are positive and absent of evil,
we take advantage of them on the spot,
seizing the moment,
never letting them escape,
as convergence is casuistic in nature,
we never know when it'll come
or if it'll ever show up again.

"It Is commonly Said That Love…"

It is commonly said
that Love is never having to say you're sorry,
and never having to apologize.

It's been said therefore,
that in this regard Love is perfect,
and as it belongs to a twosome,
it is twice perfect.

But the risk of Love without forgiveness or repentance,
is that it could turn rigid and selfish.

It's the kind of Love,
where forgiveness is replaced
by obfuscation, and solitary reprimands.

It's the kind of Love were repentance
is replaced by wounded self-esteem, offended egos and pride.

To the contrary,
Love is to know how to forgive those that we Love.

When forgiving one another,
we also forgive ourselves.

Love between two people works
only if the couple
acts in unison on everything.

So, when one fails, both fail, or maybe,
the one that has failed is the other.

Love is to be sorry together.
Love is absent of pride, selfishness,
hidden, forbidden or sacred places.

What really matters in Love
is what one feels for one another.

In Love,
it does not matter
if there is a gesture or not,
but only if whatever takes place is done from our hearts.

Love is not arrogant, Love is humble.

When in Love, complains are ill fitted,
punishment creates opaqueness, pride stains,
selfishness hurts, indifference kills.

When there is Love,
the offense is born with its own pardon,
innately attached to it.

Remorse is always done by both lovers,
and it is in this way,
that forgiveness does not exist in love.

It is not necessary to say I'm sorry
or to ask for forgiveness,
as we already possess them both,
already sculpted
in our welded hearts.

"When we Are Not Together"

I would like to know how you are doing.
Hopefully, you are as happy as I am.

I've noticed sadness in your voice,
and I would love to free you from it.

What we have together is too good
to not be rejoicing about it.
Be spontaneous, you'll always be like that.

Let us try never to be rigid.

This entire wonderful thing between us
has been like a sudden water fountain
gushing by itself without any help.

Let me be me,
I'll let you be you.

But also, Let's be us, together,
like each one of us is.

We already are pretty much alike,
and this will keep us spontaneous,
tight, while becoming closer and closer.

I would like to know how you are feeling.
I wish you could feel as close to me as I do to you.

I hope that my words are encouraging,
nor a complaint or criticism,
but supportive, and not demanding.

I would like you to feel
the strength we generate together,
and that this strength be your joy,
when we are apart.

I would like to be with you right now, and forever.

But, when we are not together,
let our couple be your carriage and shield,
and let me inspire you to be happier than ever,
that those days apart are serene and peaceful,
and go by quickly
while we wait for each other's return.

Then, as it happens in our reencounters,
we always realize in joy
that our feelings have only grown,
the couple's gotten stronger,
and our life together has become over time
better and better than ever before.

"The Soul Whispers"

Today I remembered those whispers,
And in total silence…I slid back to the past.

Those sounds that were soft and constant,
like a tiny creek, a crystalline and crisp trickle.

The soul's whispers suddenly irrupted
as we were behind the scenes.

The stage, the play, the performers, the audience
were all "acting"
as they always do,
on the other side,
putting on a show,
and living just for the "appearance" of it.

Behind the show
at the backstage of the performance,
between the drop curtains,
I could hear life…

But from afar,
I could not figure out their performance,
nor the costumes or the scenario.

The figures
from one or the other side were blurry,
I could only hear the whispers.

And without feeling it,
almost without noticing it,
it seemed as if I could even hear their souls.

The sounds of their souls
came to me as a distant whisper,
The words could not be distinguished
but only their cadence.

The people were not
what they seemed or wanted to be.
Their souls whispered something different...

Today, I remembered those whispers,
those sounds soft and constant,
like a tiny creek, a crystalline, and crisp trickle.
They were...the soul's whispers.

"Animo, Animus, Anima"

Animo, Animus, Anima, Animo, Anima..
what does it matter?
They are all one of the same.

Surprised?
Colloquially speaking,
animus is strictly associated with animosity
and all of those deeply rooted ill feelings.

But there couldn't be a more blatant misuse
of a very profound word than this!

That's why in this verse,
the word is trapped between its homonyms,
Animo, Anima that is.

Therefore,
Hereunto is the other side of Animus
or is it Animo or Anima perhaps?

Well, either or, here is what it is…

Animus is a state or a condition
that signals our "vital engagement"
into the game of life.

Animus is desire and willingness combined.
It can be an attitude towards anything or anyone
or a condition resulting from the deliberate
or even the unintended ways we live.

Animus is the impetus of the spirit,
and the spark of the soul.
It is the vital force of the heart,
the driver of our design,
the engine behind our intendment,

the catalyst of our purpose,
the vital energy behind our meaning,
the fuel for our plan,
the secret ingredient behind our courage,
the lightbulb inside our mind,
the energy behind our willingness,
the precondition to our disposition,
the paved road towards our goals.

Animus is the level of our intensity
in a state or a condition of willingness.
It lies right at our core, inside our inner spirit.

Animus also depicts the degree of our engagement in life.

If Animo, Animus, Anima is not spontaneously present
at the onset of life's endless paths,
then it is one we have to fight for,
putting our best efforts to acquire it,
in order to find "the right frame of mind"
to embark in any quest.

Are you in good "animus" today?
Are you of good "animus" everyday?
Do you have the right "animo" this morning?

Animo, Animus, Anima, What does it matter?
After all, They are all,
one of the same.

"As Time Passes"

As time passes and life goes on,
we are reminded by tragedy,
how precious life is,
and how privileged we are
to be healthy and alive.

Life is short, very short.
We shall live in full,
squeezing every drop out of each single day.

Our family, our friends are
our travel mates in this intense voyage of life.

Work and enjoyment are necessary to keep us busy,
but love is
what gives us balance and equilibrium.

As time passes and life goes on,
and the turn of the next generation approaches,
the best satisfaction is to see our descendants
living out in full blossom,
free, healthy, and successful
in whatever they do,
happy with their lives, friends, and loved ones.

"Do You Remember Those Eyes?"

Do you remember those eyes?
I do…I always will.

His eyes smiled at you,
with their little twinkle,
that tiny movement where they seemed
to close in on you,
like you were the most important person in the world,
at least at that moment to him.

And you couldn't help but feel
that you had his full attention, and respect.

His eyes read people so well,
those laser beams made you
feel so good,
high spirited,
and full of optimism,

His eyes touched you with his total approval,
giving a tremendous sense that he was professing,
and doting his unlimited faith on you.

He was a source of strength,
and was able very quickly to get close to you,
as only those
who truly accept others as they are, can.

His life was a celebration of life.
A life that is precious,
A life that because it is brief,
shall be lived in full,
squeezing every second out of it.

A life where devoting himself to others
is the best legacy he leaves behind.

Do you remember those eyes?
I do…I always will…

"For Our Children"

Let them grow, healthy and strong.
So, they discover a world
that is both difficult,
and fantastic at the same time.

Let them travel
and meet its people,
and love all their fellow life travelers
especially those in need.

And let it be that everything
they start, embark on, or get involved in,
they do it with conviction, dedication, and grit.

Let them enjoy and appreciate their parents
and an immensely happy childhood
with boundless love,
filled with dreams, illusions,
innocence candor, and imagination.

And as they grow,
let them discover
everything and everyone around them,
as it is, and as they really are.

Then, over time,
let them progressively discover who they really are,
so, they find their true selves,
just as God brough them to earth.

So, whoever they are,
they are happy, and comfortable in their own skin.

So, whatever they do, they do it well.

Hence,
from then onwards, forever,
they are always their authentic selves.

We'll teach you
to be humble, honest, and non-materialistic,
and do our best to inspire you.

We'll offer you our infinite love,
and our passion for knowledge, sports, and nature.

We'll teach you discipline
to ingrain on you a rock-solid work ethic,

We'll always push, and press,
we will be as demanding as you can bear, and then some.

We'll make you strong
while teaching you how to live in full, so,
life does not go by without you
taking full advantage of every minute of it
regardless of the circumstances.

"Destiny"

Life is a tightly wound chain of occurrences,
a maddening scramble
we cannot govern nor control.

Out future is being made
everyone one thousand of a second.

It is an infinite,
never ending, dynamic,
and totally random string of connected occurrences.

All of these intersecting events,
relate, influence, interact,
and intertwine among themselves.

Each and every event in life
is a wonderful and complex accident.
These include the finite ways of our
lives, the urgency of living,
and the uncertainty of our future.

We are an accident, every moment we are alive,
and in the end always an intricate mishap.

Life is a complicated interaction
of events of nature, human acts, and behavior,
and everything derived out of things
created by human beings,
all under the mantel of Life.

We have very little control over Life,
but if circumstances allow it,
with lots of faith and willingness,
we can reap from it,
immense happiness, goodwill, and joy.

"Life Endless Virtuous Circles"

As the sun sets and life ends,
the horizon explodes in thousands of colors.

Yellows, oranges, and reds of fire light the sky,
symbolizing the celebration
of a journey coming to an end.

As in life,
when we mourn the loss
and the departure of our loved ones
no longer with us,
total darkness soon arrives
and engulfs us in sorrow,
but not for long.

As we start to peek
and then gaze up at the firmament,
we recognize that there are still lights while we grieve,
that there are still lights in darkness
as countless stars and the moon
illuminate the entire night sky.

Soon enough, as in Life,
a bright new day approaches.

First it breaks
as a tiny ray of light on the horizon.

Shortly thereafter, a new beginning
inexorably commences out of darkness,
filled with shiny daylights and vivid hues,
a rebirth, a fresh new start,
is all painted on a brand new,
and splendorous pallet.

It all makes us realize that everything around us
is recurrent, recursive, and regenerated.

As each new day begins,
a daily renewal of the human existence takes place.

As a life gives way, a day ends,
night takes the stage, but only for a while.

As a new life soon starts,
a fresh new day breaks out,
and the lights of life
irrupt in full blast over the horizon.

"Enthusiasm"

There are few other expressions that depict better
what it means to be truly alive than enthusiasm.

The enthusiast is impregnated
with a halo of ebullient "effusivity,"
unstoppable and contagious desire,
restless and immense curiosity,
exalted and positive energy,
disarming candor and vibrant ingenuity,
to embark and go after
countless virtuous circles.

The enthusiast is possessed
with an overwhelming but refreshing impetus,
a cheerful and exuberant willingness,
an incessant and unrelenting drive
to explore, experiment
and experience anything or anyone.

For the enthusiast,
life is an infinite series
of precious bounties of probable or possible moonshots,
just waiting to be tapped.

Enthusiasm is the best antidote
to passivity, indifference, and lack of passion.

Enthusiasm is the essence
of inspiration, happiness, and true love.

Spontaneous waterfalls of goodness
are second nature to the enthusiast.

They are in reality,
-these driven and bursting vibes of positive energy-
deliberate joy-triggers
and unmistakable signals

that symbolize the magic key,
to the land of continuous happiness,
where we are graced with a mantle
of pulsating, ticking, vibrating, and palpable vitality.

A passionate and inspired life
is always soaked with enthusiasm,
which is the secret catalyst to unlock and bring
continuous joy into our existence
as we journey through life.

"Love and Success"

It is not whatsoever
about <u>success-driven-love,</u>
to the contrary,
everyone and everything in life
is about <u>love-driven-success</u>.

"Joy"

Joy is the highest level,
the ultimate attainment of happiness.

It is a virtuous elevated state
reaching "The Zenith of Contentment."

Joy occurs,
when happiness shines and sparkles,
when all is radiant and incandescent,
when we are
inundated,
impregnated,
soaked
with a sense of
absolute wholesomeness,
immense pleasure,
complete satisfaction,
and totally satiated feelings,
all emanating from within ourselves.

Some profess that
when we arrive,
while we are here,
or when we depart this world,
we are endowed and blessed with joy
directly from Heaven,
and The Creator himself.

Others believe that a minimum,
Joy must originate from a profound
and well-grounded spirituality.

Then there are those,
who are even certain,
that continuous Joy requires
"Clarity in Life"
originating from
"Coherence,"
the glue that connects in "sensical-harmony"
meaning with purpose in our existence.

In the final analysis, most certainly
Joy generates from any or all of the above.

Joy ensues
when we are alert, conscious and appreciative.
When we anticipate and emote in delight,
and when we are able
to taste, feel and realize the pleasure
of pure and simply, being alive.

Joy is inherent and immanent
to our core, very essence and nature.
Yet, joy can also be elusive,
hard to discern and visualize
as it is often clouded by poisons of the spirit
like,
Power,
Ambition,
Greed,
Envy,
Anger,
Grudges,
Material Wealth,
and the most dangerous of them all,
Our Ego.

In addition,
when we are unable to be
Caring,
Doting,
Humble,
and

Authentically Honest,
Joy is poignantly absent.

The fundamental prerequisites of Joy
are the inner peace and calmness
of finding and then being true to oneself.

Joy has nothing to do
with Character, Success or Riches,
it is about whether our "Existential Inner-Lights"
and our "Desire for Life at Its Fullest"
are Switched ON or not.

As it is essential to our existence,
Joy cannot be possessed or controlled.
Joy simply is.

The noble and sublime state of "Inspiration,"
perhaps the only source of continuous happiness,
is our secret ingredient,
our catapult,
our springboard
into the elevated thrill of Joy.

There is no predictable Joy in the future,
much less in the past.
Our masochistic minds tend
to take us to places that no longer exist
or are yet to be.
To the contrary,
Joy's eternal presence
exists only in the "Here and Now!"

A condition of permanent Joy
is the telltale of the "Wizards of Life,"
those that have lived long enough,
but still possess pure, candid, and innocent hearts.

When Joyous,
we exude,
transcend,
exult,
exhilarate,
elate,
blithe,
celebrate in exuberance,
and seemingly hover,
levitate,
float,
and waft
above mundane reality
in utter and sheer bliss.

In Joy is
where the truest,
purest meaning of life resides,
although "Hidden in Plain Sight" within.
Joy is one the biggest existential treasures
we hold while we exist and are alive.

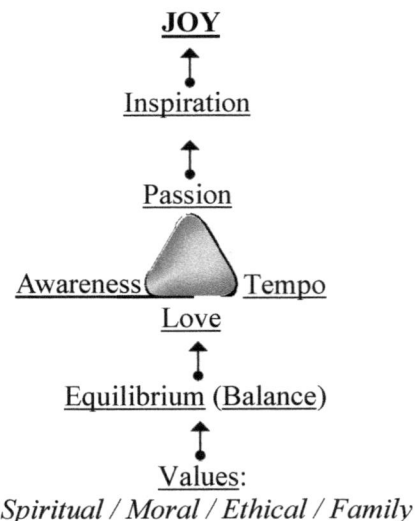

"No Longer Just A Dream"

Martin Luther King Jr. believed that society's three evils were: Militarism, Racism, and Materialism.

Today, decades later, we can easily argue that all of them remain among the biggest threats we face:
1) With events like Ukraine and ISIS we see the danger of militarism.
2) With Uvalde, Texas; Cleveland, Ohio, and Philadelphia, Pennsylvania; Charleston, South Carolina; Dayton, Ohio; El Paso, Texas; Parkland, Florida and Las Vegas, Nevada, we see the lingering poison of racism.
3) With income inequality, the lack of social mobility and the lack of a fair shot for all, we see evidence of the darker side of materialism.

And yet, today, Reverend King's dream lives on and, as the name of this play goes, it is "*No Longer Just a Dream*."

What if Dr. King could take a look, a peek into what happened to his dream? Well, according to prominent physicists, including Einstein and Goddard, time travel, at least mathematically speaking, is possible.

We are now in 1964, 56 years ago...
"Who are you?" Asks the Reverend.
"Reverend, I'm a time traveler assigned to you."
"A time traveler?"
"Yes, Sir, I've been sent straight from Heaven to track the lives of exceptional men like you."
The Reverend looks at the time traveler with total skepticism.
"I've been following you all the way, Sir, all the way, but recent events have changed my task."
"I don't have time for this. Now, if you would excuse me!"

Unfazed the time traveler quickly swipes his hand across. Dr. King's key life events flash in front of him in rapid succession.

Suddenly the scrolling of the images slows down. On the floating image, Dr. King can watch himself speak to a crowd in Selma, Alabama, in March of 1965. Dr. King states emphatically, "We can do this, we must do this, we will take their power through the vote."

Then the images scroll again, and now Reverend King speaks to an enormous crowd at the footsteps of the Lincoln Memorial in Washington D.C., they've gone backwards in time to August 28, 1968. "I have a dream...that all men are created equal..."

Then, the image fast-forwards again. In rapid succession, Dr. King is shown receiving the Nobel Peace Prize in Stockholm, Sweden; then standing next to President Johnson later in 1964, while the Commander in Chief signs the Civil Rights Act; followed by August 6, 1965, when the Reverend is witnessing the signing of the Voting Rights Act.

"Reverend King, the seeds you planted have had a profound effect on our country. I've been instructed to take you forward in time to observe what happened to your dream."

And, before the Reverend can react, the time traveler is standing with Dr. King on a barren island outside of what appears to be an abandoned one-story prison made of stone blocks.
"Where are we?"
"We are at Robben Island, Sir, it is the Alcatraz Island of Cape Town, South Africa. As you can see and feel, it's bitterly cold, humid, and windy. It's a place dammed by immense hu- man suffering, like Devil's Island in South America's French Guyana, and Auschwitz in Poland."
"Why are we here?"
"In these houses of oppression, an extraordinary man, following in your footsteps, spent the majority of a 27-year period of incarceration, imprisoned for opposing the racist system of South Africa's segregation."
"Apartheid?" "Right, Sir."

"Reverend, let me introduce you to this remarkable South African."
It is now 1993, in a place familiar to Dr. King. Overcome by emotion, one more time, he witnesses the King of Sweden presenting the Nobel Peace Prize to a tall white-haired man. Suddenly, the setting changes and they are now standing inside the South African Congress Building, in the country's Capital of Pretoria.
"Reverend, it's now May 10, 1994, and this great man is addressing the nation as he's just been elected President of South Africa. Let's listen to what he's saying."
"…This is a victory for justice, for peace, for human dignity. At last, we have achieved political emancipation. Never, never, and never again shall it be that this beautiful land experiences the oppression of one by another…the sun shall never set on such glorious human achievement, let the freedom reign, God Bless Africa."

Dr. King is at first speechless, then he states, "What a remarkable achievement, the end of Apartheid through a democratically elected member of the oppressed."
He asks, his voice trembling, "What is his name?" "Nelson Mandela."

The Reverend is in a trance, shaken to the core as he holds back blissful tears of pride. The floating image changes again and South Africa's newly inaugurated President is answering questions from the local press.
"The National Rugby Team uniforms should be changed to reflect the colors of the majority in the country," asserts a reporter.
"Absolutely not! We will respect and participate in the traditions and preferences of one another. This will not be a witch-hunt. This process is about unity and integration, and not about dominance or oppression or imposing the will of one, some or even many others."

The time traveler continues, "Reverend, in the future you become famous and revered all over the planet. Your ideas and struggles resonate all over the world. Testimonials of your life and your messages are all around us. In the United States alone, there are some 650 streets named after you. Also, there are monuments, parks and streets dedicated to you in countries like Australia, Austria, France, Germany, India, Israel, Italy, Senegal, South Africa, and Zambia among others."

In front of his eyes, the floating screen moves from place to place, showing his name across cities, countries, and continents.
"I wish I could tell you that I 'm pleased, but accolades about me are not something I particularly enjoy. I'm more interested in what happened to my ideas," states a visibly uncomfortable Dr. King.
"Well, Dr. King, your ideas and persona have grown significantly over time and Mr. Mandela is a great example of your legacy.

But the definite crystallization of many of your dreams took place years later when the improbable, the impossible and the unthinkable took place. However, to wit- ness that, we need to move closer to home," describes the time traveler as he continues, "Reverend, we are now in Chicago at the 2008 Democratic Party National Convention. Here is another remarkable man. An African American Senator launching his political career nationwide. Let's listen to what he has to say."
"How long will justice be crucified, and truth be buried? There is no blue or red, black, or white, native, or Hispanic, liberal, or conservative America, there is the United States of America."
The Reverend is visibly impacted by his words, then asks, "Who's he?"
"A Harvard graduate, Sir, specialized in constitutional law, son of a Kenyan man and an American woman from the mid-west, who was raised in Hawaii and Indonesia. He's married to a Harvard and Yale graduate, and they have two daughters."
"What's his name?" "Barack Obama."

"Reverend, let me take you forward a bit to January 2009, but let me prepare you, Sir, it's going to be emotional, very emotional for you."
The Reverend sees a familiar image, they are standing on the footsteps of the Lincoln memorial, right in front of him he can see the D.C. mall running through the Washington obelisk all the way to the Capitol. As with his very own speech in the same place 45 years earlier, there is a huge crowd gathered. He realizes though, that they are all facing in the opposite direction towards The US Congress, also, the crowd is much, much larger than his was.

"Why are they all here?"
"Let's get closer and find out, Reverend."
Facing the immense crowd from the opposite end, they are now standing on a stage built on top of the footsteps and in front of the US Congress building. Amazed Dr. King realizes that the multitude extends all the way to the Lincoln memorial. The elevated and sizable stage is filled with people. The Reverend does not recognize anyone but picks up what the ceremony is about right away.
"Why are we here?" He asks.
Then, as Senator Barack Obama stands up and places his hand on Lincoln's bible, a bolt of emotion overcomes the Reverend, sending chills down his spine. His lower lip trembles, his stare is intense and teary at the same time. He is rendered speechless with a tight knot in his throat.
"I Barack Obama, swear to uphold..."
"Yes, we can... oh Lord, we did it, we did it with the power of the vote," states a visibly overwhelmed Dr. King.
A new image quickly flashes and is familiar to him. With a broad smile in amazement, the Reverend observes:
"So, as Mandela and me, he also received the Nobel Peace Prize."
Then before he can act, they have switched to January 2013, while still standing at the same stage on top of the footsteps of Congress. The scene repeats itself as the oath of office is taken. Dr. King realizes that Obama's hair is now sprinkled with white. He pauses and then it hits him.
"Re-elected?" The Reverend blurts out. "How could that have happened?"
"Well, Reverend, he's a symbol and a fruit of your success. A more than worthy successor to what you started. Remarkably, Sir, he's been elected both times by almost half of the country's 72% white majority, and by a large percentage of the country's Asian, African American, and Hispanic population. The whites were the clinchers though, they elected him both times, Sir."

They are now in Cairo, Egypt. President Obama is speaking.
"Let's listen to his speech, Reverend."
"For centuries, black people in America suffered the lash of the whip as slaves and the humiliation of segregation. However, it was not violence that won full and equal rights. It was peaceful and determined

insistence upon ideals..., a tradition that has stretched from the days of the country's founding to the civil rights movement, a tradition based on the simple idea that we all have a stake in one another, and that what binds us together is greater that what drives us apart. That if enough people believe in the truth of the proposition and act on it, then, we might not solve every problem, but we can get something meaningful done."

Dr. King is overwhelmed and yet relieved as he stares in the horizon, His face projects a sense of intense satisfaction, realization, and pride. "It happened, it really happened," he says in a trance. "Well, Sir, to a large degree, yes. but there's still a lot of
work to do. Let me show Reverend."
Then the images of the shootings in Orlando, Ferguson, and Charleston flash by.
"I see," says a circumspect Reverend, then he asks, "How did the President react?"
"Let's go there," says the time traveler.
"Violence is a dead end. We will extend a hand if you unclench your fist," President Obama states.
"We still have a long way to go," declares the Reverend.
"That's true, Reverend, but your dream is not just that any longer, it is now a reality."

Author's commentary

1) The Quibbler and The Street Juggler

- In life one has to juggle to be in balance, but in order to be able to do so, endless practice and learning are required. Both will provide the knowledge, experience, and self-confidence to execute impossible feats fearlessly and flawlessly. Just as with the quibbler, we'll always be surrounded by ignorance and pessimism. The naysayers will be out there until our results overwhelm them. But one can never forget that in order to maintain balance it takes continuous hard work.
- In life, there are alternating forces pulling and throwing us into extremes, causing a flow that gravitates like a pendulum or a metronome ticking from one extreme to another.
- Freedom lies within you. Balance is being free within life's pendulum, as within the swings of a metronome.

2) The Equilibrist

"Are we all equilibrists?"
"No, but we all should seek to be like one."
"Besides not falling from a tightrope into excesses, why should we?"
"Balance is one the foundations of happiness."
"Is balance the true message underlying this writing?"
"Yes, as so is inner freedom."
"Why inner freedom?"
"Inner freedom is perilous because it begins within you. To exercise and sustain it requires self-confidence that only experience, and knowledge can provide. There is no truer expression of the power of inner freedom that the performance of an acrobat, since he or she must not only thrive on it, but also during the performance calls on it for strength. In final analysis, we are the ones who inside have to be free."

3) The Balloon Salesman

- No matter what others think, to dream is to contemplate life through magical magnifying glasses. Dreamers are like wizards.
- Some of us live on a balloon all the time and that's a wonderful gift.

"Why does the world of dreams belong almost exclusively to children?"
"That is the challenge for every adult, isn't it?"
"Do people simply stop dreaming as they grow old?"
"Yes, they do as they let unfiltered reality control their ability to feel and wish."
"Is a life without dreams void of color?"
"Yes, it is one lived while stuck at ground level, is a dull and sour life."
"Do dreams make you happy?"
"Of course, they do! Inspiration and blissfulness are required in order to dream, and both are a couple of the most essential ingredients of happiness."

"When I dream my mind is not in control?"
"When you dream, your brain is nothing but a silent wit- ness and an archive of your life's memories, out of where your imagination pulls out all the content required for your dreaming activities."

4) The Boy in the Picture

- Always remember this, nothing or no one can stop you from dreaming. When you dream you visualize how you want to shape your future and there are no limits or boundaries to what it achievable or possible.

5) The Gift of Life

- Resilience is a virtue that carries you through any hard- ship or obstacle, and if you make it part of your core, weaving it into your essence and your nature, it'll never leave you.
- Every challenge, grievance or pain, every obstacle or mountain to climb has a counteraction to resolve.
- You never sit still waiting for things to happen. You should never fail to react. In the overall scheme of things, we are accountable for the gift of life. Our actions always have to reflect our eternal gratitude for being here.

6) The Unwavering, Unflickering, Tiny Little Flame

- What drives resilience is our own inner flame. When we learn to recognize and harness this, it provides us with indomitable strength.

7) The Magic in Life

"All I have to do is love life?"
"Love yourself, love others, love life and all of it will become magical, or rather, a magical miracle for you."

8) The Blue Unicorn

- In life we all need those really special people that bring out the best in us.
- In life our blue unicorns only exist if can see them.

9) A Song in The Rain

> "Can we see beauty when in pain? Can we hear music in spite of loss or tragedy?"
> "Can we contemplate adversity with respect, but without fear?"
> "Can we be right in the center of a storm and truly believe it will pass?"

- If you can hear and feel music despite the rain, then not only you can overcome anything that comes your way, but you can also enjoy it even in the direst of circumstances.

10) Way, Way Up There

- One way to look at the unintended, often unexpected departure of our loved ones, is to realize that their spiritual presence and memories stay with us forever.

11) A Strong Group of Few

- The courage and sacrifices of the few, lie behind all the freedoms we enjoy.

12) The Land of The Happy People

- Be careful! Angry individuals are everywhere, and they are like body snatchers that can grab you at any time. Also be mindful of anger itself, as it can overtake you at any moment, poisoning your ability to be happy.

- Ask yourself, why Today of all days, they, he, or she rattled you? Why did you notice anger in all of those people? Why not yesterday or the day before? After all, each and every day they have the same temperament. Besides, was it necessarily their anger what you detected, or perhaps your own?
- You see, how easy the anger of others can affect you. It all depends on one's attitude and the kind of lenses we wear when contemplating and judging others.

13) The Spinning Wheel of Life

"Is life circuitous then?"
"Not exactly, think about your circles in life as the trajectory of the wake you leave behind. What was, is and will be again. Everything that occurs to you has already happened millions of times before and will happen again! In life everything comes around in full circle. We either draw upon well-lived circles or not, thus we may as well strive to be happy, to live a gentle, blissful, and inspired life, always following the better instincts of our hearts."

14) Hope

- Hope is the best source of inner-strength and freedom.

"Does hope represents how I'll never give up on anything?"
"There are times in life when we'll have to let go. Hope though is totally different. To begin with, it's how your innate attitude is supposed to feel. Thus, when you go after some- thing, do it with passion, but always driven by the strength and resolve that hope gives you. So, it's not that you never give up, it's that you never lose hope enabling you to never give up."
"Why is always hope the last freedom standing?"
"Even in the face of great tragedy and hardship, through the loss of everyone and everything, nothing or no one can ever deprive you of your ability to hope."

15) An Inspired Life

- Take stock of your life and realize how much happiness you have going for you.
- Don't block your own way. Now is the time for you to spread your wings and fly. Seize the moment and grab by the horns, what life offers you. Whatever rattles you from within, pursue it with all your heart. Capture and be grateful at the same time for every moment and everything that is conveyed to you, especially all that you earn through hard work.
- To be inspired is a state, a condition which you are driven to with grace and nobility by a sublime and overwhelming desire to live, to achieve and be happy. Inspiration harnesses all your best endowments into a highly functional state that brings out the absolute best in you.
- You should pursue inspiration in your life. It'll provide you with continuous happiness.

16) The Past and The Future

- You can't control what others feel or how they behave.
- Day by day, each person writes their own life pages in indelible ink in a book that entirely theirs.
- There's futility in not letting go, getting stuck in the past and not being able to move on.

"What's the difference between the past and the future catching up?"
"One catches up with you for things you did, the other for the things you failed to do."

- We need to learn and treasure our past, but never be a slave to it. Too many of us live 'ever after' consumed by things that no longer exist, things that are otherwise long gone, but linger in the tortuous masochist and narrow, very narrow corridors and labyrinths of our minds.

- You have to live now! Do not skip a day, do not delay what you can do Today. Do it free from negative fantasies that remain from the past.

17) Reach Out

"What about if 'moving on' is not enough to cure a grudge?"
"Holding grudges will keep us stuck in the past on endless loops of pain. When you give, you should always do so despite the behavior of others, as it'll make your deeds not only genuine, but it'll allow your independence. Your actions won't be conditioned by how others respond to you."

18) Winning Is Not for The Faint of Heart

"So, I don't necessarily win against an opponent?"
"That's right, human beings are not always the adversaries. Life is actually filled with obstacles, challenges, difficulties even tragedies, some of them seemingly insurmountable, that only the attitude of a winner can defeat."
"Do I need to know how to win to be able to navigate the perils of life?"
"Absolutely! You need an indomitable desire and will to triumph. It is a key ingredient in order to be able to withstand and conquer whatever life throws at you or whatever you set as your goals."

19) Self-Reliance

- In life, don't expect or even desire that things be handed to you. Just hold on firmly to the belief that you have to earn it.

"Do you mean that caring and empathy for others is something that I could decide to pour my heart into, but its foundations will originate only from my own self- reliance?"
"Right. Self-reliance and individualism are often confused with selfishness. Actually, self-reliant people, even as they depend on themselves, can still be fully dedicated to helping

others in need. Self-reliance or first prioritizing one-self has nothing to do with and is not incompatible at all with giving."
"But I do rely on others all the time."
"Of course, you do, but you must rely on yourself first."

20) The Better Instincts of The Heart

- On matters of love, wisdom is our guiding light. It sprinkles our better instincts of the heart, our feelings, and our passions with a love compass. It answers or shortcuts countless love crossword puzzles that we may have to solve.
- The better instincts of our heart are always right. Follow them without hesitation. They are one of the keys to a blissful life.

21) Life is Bliss (The Importance of the Small Details in Life)

- Love grows out of little things. Love is captured through small gestures. Love is preserved and made out of teeny, tiny details that we give and receive, to and from one another.
- Always follow your heart.

    "But how do I go about it?"
    "Perhaps by understanding what being blissful is all about. If you do, rest assured that you'll be able to act on your feelings, while in possession of precious knowledge on perhaps one of the most important treasures in matters of love."
    Focus on giving with all your heart, but mind carefully who you are giving to, as to what makes little details resonate, is their catalyst, empathy.

22) Love's Rabbit Hole

- Your rabbit is that person you want to spend the rest of your life with.

23) The Secret Lies in Opposite Ends Working Together Forever

- Take stock of your life as a couple. That's your treasure. The certificate of authenticity. The truth about how good your life together really is or isn't.

24) What is Love?

- The untamable feelings of longing, desire, admiration, and respect for each other. It is that person with whom we aspire to feel safe, protected and never alone.

25) What is True Love?

- Always remember, true love is not driven by success, nor does it disappear in failure. When it does arrive, it stays with you forever.

26) The Three-Legged Stool

- And, if indeed, true love finds you, always remember that those three legs of the stool, all need to be present for the couple to last and remain happy.
- There are three separate but interconnected dimensions to a couple: Friendship, Passion, and Love. Each one requires hard work. Each is distinctively different, but equally important. All serve as both the engines and foundations of a continuously happy, genuinely solid and, therefore, lasting union.

27) Sorting Out the Rest

- We all need tutelage in life. Find yourself a wise mentor that can guide you through the mine fields of existence.

28) If I Could Find You Out There

- Let me caution you, after a breakup one has to be especially wary of falling in love when on the rebound. When driven by wealth and success, your heart can be easily fooled.
- Such passions are not genuine, just mere infatuations, impregnated with the emptiness of material things. Instead of the security and comfort they are supposed to provide, they only offer you sadness and solitude. You become comfortably unhappy, especially when you are all alone at night with your own pillow.

29) A Labor of Love

- There are mental an emotional issues, some are diseases that are beyond our control and require professional care, even therapy. The challenge is to recognize and accept them whether in ourselves or others, we always praise, recognize, and respect such difficult feats.

30) There Is a Life to Be Lived Out There

- Very few appreciate how ephemeral true love can be. However, life goes on. As you long for and treasure what you had and still want, as you start piling-up regrets that swallow the precious and scarce time remaining in planet earth, wake up! There is still life to be experienced and enjoyed out there!
- So go out and live. Don't cut yourself any slack. Life does not occur while on the sidelines.
- In final analysis, we all want to be happy, hence it behooves us to crack the riddle of Joy. Rest assured that the key to solving is never to be detached, but just the contrary, is to be absolutely involved and immersed in your life.

31) Life's True Success Is to Be Happy

- Your life's clock is ticking. Your life's battery is wasting always.

- You don't want to wake up one morning and realize that, just like that, your life is coming to an end.

32) The Happiness Formula

- For happiness to ensue in life, there are three simultaneous attitudes to pursue: Passion, Tempo, and Awareness.
- Then, there are three supporting blocks needed for it to last, namely: Love, Balance and Values.
- There is a noble hypersensitive state that this ecosystem of virtuous attitudes and supporting blocks creates: And that is Inspiration, perhaps the only source of continuous happiness.

33) Optimism

- Optimism is a deliberate attitude that, if not born with, or if it's not our natural inclination, we must learn or teach ourselves to embrace, practice and carve it into our spirits making it second nature to our persona.
- Always remember that optimism is the key to opening many of life's doors, those that only the optimist can see, the kind of places and outcomes only an optimist can reach, experience, and enjoy.
- In the game of life, optimism, more often than not, contains the only winning hand.

34) Small Sacrifices

- At some point in time, circumstances will inexorably occur when life will demand we sacrifice for others in need. It'll be up to us to live up to this, and the payback is the gift of a fulfilling life.

35) Of Fate and Fairy Tales

- Life's fairy tales first reside inside each one of us.

36) My Radiant Goddess of The Night

- What could be more romantic than being with our other half on a deserted beach with a slight breeze blowing and a star-studded night sky?

37) There Is Something About You

- Make a point of recognizing and being aware of all those special little things about your loved ones that make you happy.

38) Life, Character, and Virtue

- Character and Virtue are not God given gifts that you are born with. To the contrary, they require hard and persistent work in order to build, grow, acquire, and preserve them.
- Your virtues define your character. Your character determines your legacy.
- Character sits at the confluence between what others think, and what we, deep inside really think about ourselves.
- Being virtuous, besides being an essential component of a wholesome character, not only needs to be acquired and developed, but at the same time, in order to overcome, sustain, outlast, and endure our existence, is the essential tool we depend on.

39) Snap (Snap Out of It)

- More often than not, we are our own worst enemies. Somehow, somewhere, we manage to get in our own way. Sabotaging our existential paths and roads.

- Snapping out of it, is a tool that teaches us how to avoid self-defeating behaviors. It's not about snapping and losing control, but exactly the opposite. It's about awakening to regain control of yourself and the circumstances or situations you may be in.

- Think of it as a safety mechanism, an emergency brake that halts you right at the start, preventing anything from even commencing. The idea is that you catch yourself, before you find yourself in whatever world you are about to fall into, especially one where you are your very own worst enemy.
- Extricate yourself and disengage from the situation by freezing it. Stepping back, snapping out of it, allows for perspective of facts from the outside and enables the day, circumstance, and road ahead, to be clear and free of your own persona, blocking and perhaps even self-sabotage.

40) The Chimney Sweep

- We all need sweeping to free up our spirits, enabling us to dream, fly far away and high up, into the deepest confines of the universe.
- We all need to make a deliberate effort to constantly cleanse our spirits, in order for our dreams to fly unimpeded.

41) Faith

- Use Faith as a source of inner strength. It will teach you not only to believe, but also to see through any obstacles life may present. To neutralize and overcome doubt, indecisive- ness and especially fear, Faith is the best source. The more Faith you profess, the more you grow as a person.
- Faith is the strongest, deepest, most indomitable, and unbreakable of all beliefs. It'll carry you through the most profound of all sorrows and pain, through devastating losses and period of weakness, through storms and shattering quakes.
- Faith enables you to forgive with grace and be giving with- out expecting rewards or gratitude.

- Faith grants you a benevolent heart, a driven spirit, a calm, kindred, and meaningful soul. As we profess it, walking alongside The Creator, Faith is always pure and genuine. "Is Faith exclusive for any particular religion?"

  "Religion is the most important known method, though not the only one, when we practice Faith. We profess Faith for our partner, our loved ones, humanity, our friends, and others."

- Faith is practiced by all religions. Faith is the driving force underlying all of them. Inner Faith lies, ready to be lit and provide us with a glowing celestial halo that emanates from within.
- As with all The Faiths in the world, a good analogy to think could be that we all breath earth's air from the same source and in the same way in spite of our differences.

42) Whispering at Your Heart

- We shall seek to whisper to our loved ones. So as to not to drown their hearts with noise, we seek enchantment through a soft cadence of words. We whisper love incantations. We whisper at their heart.

43) Life, Evolution and Change Among Us

- Machiavelli said, "If you want to see people at their worst, bring them changes."
- Our fear to change, causes the building of roadblocks and excuses on our existential paths. All of this is based on false perceptions of comfort and safety. These are simply artificial obstacles that we can wipe out in an instant. Change is always there and one turn away.
- A wholesome life resides in the power of change, as we constantly renew and reinvent ourselves. Don't be afraid of it, embrace it.

44) Life Wizards

- Life wizards have candid and innocent intentions emanating from their hearts. They love life and smile at everyone. They have playful souls and don't take anything or anyone too seriously. They are the ones we seek for safe harbor in the direst of circumstances. For them every moment and all people are precious and irreplaceable. They always have a sunny disposition and possess the secret of how to be continuously happy.

45) Life as a Journey

- The sheer power, force, and intensity of the oceans and many of its elements were elevated in Greek mythology to levels of God and Goddesses of the sea. They believed that's how powerful they were. That's why, as in life, we never go against the ocean, to the contrary we harness or absorb its energy to facilitate our journey.
- Through the course of our lives, we are all embarked on a never ending perilous and highly rewarding voyage. In order to have a safe passage you have trust your vessel. Above all, it's always pertinent to remember that our existential realization and joyful ride resides mainly in the journey, not the destination.

46) Of Wealth, Fame, and Love

- What is austerity to wealth?
- What is anonymity to fame?
- What is freedom to love?
- Do we sacrifice some for the benefit of others?

47) Of Family, True Friendship and Love

- Regarding family, true friendship and love, we are like Dumas' three Musketeers, 'all for one and one for all.' The catalogue of everything we are supposed to do and want to be, is dense and comprehensive but in no instance reflects or grants the right of us to govern these three constituencies.

48) One Verse at Poet's Row

- A nascent poet surrounded by other poets. Autumn at Central Park. His true love strolling along the pond, strawberry fields, and poet's row. On the spur of the moment, inspiration bursts out.

49) Life as a Circus

- Most, if not all the characters of a circus inhabit each one of us. At a minimum we have a bit of each one of them inside. For some, we were literally born as one of the circus per- formers.
- The challenge then is, what are we? A ring master or an equilibrist? A trapezist or a juggler? A clown or a magician? Discovering this out and mastering it, is the key for a great performance in life's circus.

"Do we choose who we want to be in life?"
"To a degree yes, but to a degree no. We are born with a series of aptitudes that indicate what we should aim to mas- ter. You will never be a trapezist in a circus simply because you want to. You will be one if you have the natural ability coupled with a strong desire and an intense, relentless, and continuous effort to master it. In the end, given those three premises, you will be a proficient trapezist undertake."
"Why compare life to a circus?"
"To contemplate life as a circus is an exercise in wisdom. Life's circumstances present themselves pretty much in the same way all these characters in the circus do when they perform. On the other hand, the extreme activities and planned mayhem in the three rings under a tent, symbolize at the same time, hard earned virtuosity and masterfully executed talent."

- To perfect one or several of the characters of a circus, is to master life when it comes to comparable circumstances. Plenty of our lives' feats are pure and simple, acts of magic or balance, juggling or taming, acrobatics or clowning, ring mastering and even simply just those of being patrons.

50) Those Shiny Curls of Mine

- Sailing calm seas while riding a gentle breeze, the young poet recites words of love as if he is painting a magnificent canvas filled with the precious colors of an infatuated heart.

51) Clarity in Life

- Life is always in constant motion. Lingering negatives are simply incompatible with the dynamics of being truly alive.
- In Korean culture they define certain kinds of pain as unresolved sorrows. This philosophy is known as "Han." There are losses and tragedies that we acknowledge and accept.
- Accepting the fact that these type of pain and sorrows will come and go, we don't hide, ignore, or try to avoid them. To the contrary, we recognize their existence facing the fact that they are not going away. We are aware that the pain will subside as we put them in their proper place, and we don't allow them to control or drive our lives.

"What to do when regrets and sorrows want to take a hold of us?"
"When you feel them coming, or when you realize that you've fallen into any of those states, first of all breath slowly and deep, and as you inhale, spell the word LIFE in your mind. Then, exhale while saying LIFE and visualize the word spreading throughout you. Repeat this until angst subsides. It works wonders."

52) Contemplating Your Face

- We can appreciate our partner's face outer beauty like no one else because it radiates his or her many life experiences, "lived" in tandem with us.

53) Gratitude

- Practice expressing the following to your loved ones: Being alive and having you are precious and irreplaceable gifts that I have to earn every day. Let us thank The Creator. Let us thank our existence.

54) Always There

- True Love is always there. Always is. Always will be. If you don't let it go, it Never Fails!

55) A Good Riddle

- We don't have to solve every mystery and answer every question. Life's time span is short, hence precious. There is no time to be wasted.

56) Doubt

"Why are doubts so pervasively nagging?"
"It is easy to sit down, commiserate, doubt everything and every- one, and do nothing. More often than not, doubts without its three antidotes are just fake walls built out of lame excuses. So always remember, when in doubt apply: Trust, Method, or Purpose."

- When you apply Trust to doubt, you neutralize it. When you apply Method to doubt by sticking to discipline and the verification of facts, you overwhelm it. When you confront doubt with Purpose and goals, you crush it.

57) Duality

- Sometimes in life we tend to view people, the world and life itself, as choosing between opposites. We cannot see but two options and we obsess about taking one or another. Thus, we become trapped by our existence. We contemplate everything as a duality of choices of "a" or "b." In this fashion we push ourselves into a corner and see no other alternative but to pick what we believe are the only choices available to us.

"How are duality and doubt related?"
"They are closely linked. Doubt surges-out from our ability to decide between choices, extremes, or absolutes, and our incapacity to see the middle ground, thus allowing an escape from duality."
"Before any of us individuals can seek and embrace the middle ground, doesn't society have to evolve first?"
"Certainly, our civilization has to reach a different and higher level of social behavior and belief systems to evolve out of the duality-driven environment that we are currently in. This type of evolution is not only needed but is our next societal developmental stage, and is even pointed out to us, by the field of science. For example, the next frontier in information technology is Quantum computing. Not coincidentally, at present, the computer world is based on the binary system of ones and zeros. Only two choices! To the contrary, Quantum computing is all based on a third state, where the ones and the zeros simultaneously coexist at the same time —the computer world middle ground— a kind of trinary system (Qubits), that exponentially multiplies the processing power of a computer."

58) Geniality

- All of us inside have a Genius. Our challenge is to recognize, learn and then use the best talents and abilities we were born with. Geniality taps and deploys the best of what we've got inside -whatever that may be. Our genie in the bottle is our genius. The genius is waiting to emerge. What are we waiting for?

59) Adversity

- What happens when we encounter Adversity? Have we been taught how to react, handle and cope with it? Do we prepare or are ready for it? What about the end game? Let's say for example, that Adversity strikes, and we overcome it, then what follows?
- Adversity is an intrinsic part of life. It is at the same time the ultimate challenge for everyone and everything we hold dear.
- Adversity always presents an opportunity to produce something good, even great, by overcoming it.
- It is a double-edged sword though. Hardship on one side and a door opening for renewal or a new beginning on the other.
- We confront adversity by treating it like an enemy of war.

60) How is it That You Make Me Feel So Special?

- Only you make me feel this way, no one else, you and only you.

61) Coherence (Figuring Things Out in Life)

- At some point in time, while looking for coherence, hopefully sooner rather than later, we all must, decipher our lives. What do we want out of life? What does life mean to us? What is our purpose while we are here on our magnificent earth? Coherence is one of the key existential tools that enables us to comprehend life.
- The glue that holds everything together for it to make sense, is coherence.
- Always remember, in order for us to solve things, they have to make sense, and this is possible through coherence.
- Coherence connects in "sensical-harmony" our purpose with our meaning in life.

62) Virtue

- Over a prolonged period of time, virtuosity is only achieved with a deliberate and disciplined effort.
- There is no path to virtuosity without a preceding stage of self-recovery.

63) Forgiveness

- We parents fool ourselves with the illusion that our kids don't perceive things. How mistaken we are. Our kids don't miss a beat. They see and record everything. In many situations, they even understand things —intuitively speaking— better than we do.
- Every word, every action, every display that affects our loved ones, has consequences. All inexorably wait in the future, as sooner or later they eventually catch up to us.
- Forgiving is simultaneously both empowering and liberating.
- Forgiveness is one of the most powerful weapons in the march through life and resolves emotional anchors and roadblocks.
- Don't block your own way. Move forward! The trigger for this is to forgive oneself first. That's how everything in life restarts and renews itself.

64) Silence in The Music

- In the music of life, look for silence. If you find it, you'll reach a higher existential level.

65) Reciprocity

- One of the essential elements of a fulfilling life is reciprocity. It is all in the give and take. More often than not, we focus on what we need or want to obtain, but not enough on what we have to give, which is really where we must begin. Our search for identity must include our proactive measuring of a generous mutuality and predisposition. Whatever it is that you want or

- expect from life or others, it'll only happen on a continuous basis, after you learn how to reciprocate.
- The actions of others define them. Their deeds reflect who they really are. Your actions define who you are, and not them. So, don't let their actions define you. Rise above the fray with profound maturity, sealing them in a box, so you can pour your heart into helping others regardless of their behavior.
- That's the heart of reciprocity. One doesn't act based on expecting something in return, nor does one give on the condition of being a beneficiary in return.
- From the moment you start your day, all the way until the moment you retire, the word reciprocity must reside within each one of you. What you give is exactly what you'll receive. In the long run, nothing is reciprocated, without giving!

66) Defiance

- In life sometimes we have to rise to the occasion, defying the circumstances and the odds. There are moments when we have to defy fate and stand up affirming our readiness to not surrender.
- Defiance is a stance we take in life when we need to confront and oppose adversity, hardship and especially fate, driven by the right and just reasons.

67) Curiosity

- When we have or want to learn, find out or uncover anything in life, curiosity is indispensable.

68) Decisions

- Always remember that worst decisions are those we never take. With their absence, we are simply not life participants.

69) Resilience

- A virtue to succeed or overcome whatever it is that is ahead of us is resilience.
- Resilience is intrinsic to the sacred, as a propelling force for those, who defend the truth, honor, honesty, family, and their loved ones. It is also a driving force for taking a stand on principle, ideology, religious beliefs, ethnicity, nation, their country, or their social group. Resilience is also part of the more mundane aspects of life, where we chase dreams, passion, and ideas, also of those who commit or have a duty to provide, respect, defend and love.
- Resilience is as well crucial to more pragmatic life actions, where we chose to plan, build, deliver, comply, and finish.

70) Life, Beauty, and Art

- If we are able to perceive, create and enjoy both Art and Beauty, we are genuinely experiencing life at its fullest.

71) What an Amazing Day This Is!

- Look around. Peek inside. You are composed of and surrounded by awesomeness! Everywhere, everyone, every- thing in life is simply amazing.

72) Serenity, Courage, and Wisdom

- Serenity occurs when your spirit and soul are in absolute peace. Life is supposed to be experienced through constant debates where we try to make sense of people and things. We engage in challenging arguments, where we question the coherence of our actions, life's meaning while alive, our purpose in life, as well as the knowledge that has been imparted to us. Serenity, Courage, and Wisdom are required in order to face life this way.

- Serenity, Courage, and Wisdom are all virtues of character. Serenity engenders courage while wisdom utilizes them both.

73) The Fable of The Old Young Man and The Jester

- The Jester's discovery was to realize that because he had made it such, life for a passing moment became a fairy tale. He realized that the fairy tale resided in him. It already inhabited his spirit and soul. By making others laugh, his natural inclination and greatest existential ability, was to make out of every possible moment or situation, a real-life fairy tale.

74) Symbiosis

- The fusion of love and a twosome into one.

75) The Case of The Curious Child and The Restless Magician

- Prejudice blinds us. It impedes or hampers our ability to appreciate things in life.

76) By the Hand of The Scribbler

- Writing driven by inspiration is Art.

77) What an Amazing Blessing Being Together Is

- Count your blessings each and every single day of your life if you've found your soul mate.

78) As to How Love Lights Up Everything

- Search for the beautiful light of love. Seek to be illuminated by it. Once you find it, thank The Creator.

79) When I Write to You

- Writing just for you every part of me is exposed.

80) Convergence

- Seek confluence. That's how some of life's most transcendental events take place.

81) It Is Commonly Said That Love...

- True Love does not apologize.
- True Love always forgives.
- True Love doesn't ask for it either.

82) When We Are Not Together

- While alive, there is no more difficult challenge to True Love than being apart.
- The strength of the coupling though, lies in the commitment, intensity, and authenticity of the couple's mutual feelings.

83) The Soul Whisperings

- The great comedy of life, including its participants, comes to us in the form of soul whisperers.

84) Animo, Animus, Anima

- Talk about the colloquial butchering of a word. When researching the etymology of the word animus, the following words are associated with it: Spirit, heart, design, intendment, purpose, meaning, plan, courage, mind, willingness, vital force, vital engagement, and vital energy. All of them are the complete opposite to the common use of the word.

- To achieve or get anywhere in life, this attitude or condition is essential for us.

85) As Time Passes

- Tick, tick, tick. Don't waste a precious second of your life.

86) Do You Remember Those Eyes?

- Was it the intensity? Perhaps the energy or simply life bursting-out?
- There are eyes and or stares that are simply memorable and unforgettable.

87) For Our Children

- Always celebrate your children. They crave your love, guidance, and attention. Define what you aspire of them? Under- stand what do they have a propensity for?
- Create a path, a road ahead, a wish list that charts a course until they reach adulthood.

88) Destiny

- We are our own destiny. It is on us to make it happen.

89) Life Endless Virtuous Circles

- Through clarity, coherence, virtue and balance in life, these types of circles move upward.

90) Enthusiasm

- Impetus, inspiration, joyful-desire, eager-willingness, blissful-zeal.

91) Love and Success

- Love-driven success is where True Love resides.

92) Joy

- The pinnacle of happiness at its best originates in inspiration.

93) No Longer Just A Dream

- Over time M.L.K.s' dream has inexorably become closer and closer to a working reality.
- The reflections and lessons of The Equilibrist series seek to show the path towards a life like that of M.L.K.

Poetry in Equilibrium

Parting words by the Author,

The story behind the creation of the first volume of The Equilibrist series:

Sometimes timely gifts come in minute packages. I sincerely hope this is the case with The Equilibrist series. In particular, I feel compelled to share the story about how the first volume was created, as it portrays the many shades of the human condition. The art behind the crafting of this book goes beyond anecdotical tribulations, circumstances, or the environment, these three are another worthy tale yet to be told. But the where, what, and who are not what shaped these writings.

This magical scribble became art because of how it ensued as if guided by absolutely nothing rational but just my core raw essence, unfiltered even exposed.

The Equilibrist is very intimate to me because, unintentionally, I was able to express myself through written words in ways that I always dreamed about. It is the book I always wanted to write, the checkmark on my bucket list "write a meaningful book." Irrespective of its subsequent resonance or not, the journey to create it was a once in a lifetime experience. Its completion was a moment of great personal satisfaction as I realized that feelings, dreams, wisdom, all, literally fused with words becoming pure and simply Art.

It all began with little poems, short essays that I would visualize in my head, sometimes a word here or there, some others a short phrase or even the entire idea. There was no pattern or deliberate effort. Neither could I clearly discern the stimuli that provoked them. It was just myself reacting to life as it was happening right in front of me through magnifying glasses filtered by my beliefs and wisdom.

These inspirational writings accumulated over a three-year period into a pile. As I constantly revisited it, I started to realize that somehow, I was drawing a full circle of life describing life subjects and addressing themes that reflected how I felt and deeply perceived life's journey. More and more I could visualize the difference between the stack and other forms of writing.

During the same period, as an aspiring author, I wrote numerous novels where plots and characters where created for entertainment purposes only. I wrote them all in total control of the scripts as I tweaked, changed, and polished the storylines, making fiction fit better into reality. This was a seemingly endless mechanical process that I called perfection by attrition. Towards this end, I was creating better and better book products, neatly packaged and ready for consumption.

The stack of poems was different. I'd no control over it. It just continued to grow steadily through a series of inspirational moments. Night after night, the stack kept on staring at me as I tried to figure out, where was this particular creative process going?

Then one good day I knew it was done. Don't ask me how. I just knew. Hence, the natural question was, "What is this?", "is it just a collection of poems and short essays?" I asked myself, "the pictures in an exhibition syndrome" I answered, as we seldom get to know what the artist was feeling or thinking. What we usually get, are only the pictures hanging on a wall, while we are left to speculate about it. How much better it would feel if the artist's views on their art could be present. It would result in a fantastic guiding light that will enrichen immensely the art experience, regardless of whether we would agree with the artist or not."

With these two building blocks, the stack of poems and the determination not to present another "pictures in an exhibition" poems, and essays book, I asked myself what did I want to do about them? The answer was, "I don't know. I don't have a clue."

A couple of months went by, then unexpectedly, one memorable day, literally driven by the hand of God, I simply started to reminiscence back in time, revisiting all those people and places that since I was a young child, have been magical to me. That's when the dam broke, and I started to write my narrative in earnest. From the beginning, in no particular order, the story weaved itself perfectly through the stack. One by one, the poems and essays fit as if they were predestined. At every instance, it was surreal and emotional. Each one dropped into place as if it'd always been there, awaiting them.

In the end, as opposed to pure fiction, the story was an entire compilation made up of me, including the symbols, little things and journey companions I'd encountered in life. It all happened subconsciously and in the form of art. None of it was overly obvious, not even factually the same, but as a series of brief and significant moments that had profound meaning and purpose in my own life. So much for a little book of just a few pages. I hope you all enjoy The Equilibrist series as much as I did when creating it and as I have continued to do so.

Finally, every word of The Equilibrist series was created with my family as my north star. I continuously gazed at it for inspiration and light. I know they'll easily see through the art and will rejoice the journey through the equilibrist as they will do it while walking alongside me as their guide and companion.

Erasmus Cromwell-smith II.

Poetry in Equilibrium

Acknowledgment,

This poetry book could not have been possible without the unwavering support of my ad-hoc pseudo editor's committee. Once more, your feedback was invaluable, your enthusiasm highly inspiring and your engagement, emotionally rewarding. To my team, Amy, Alfredo, Andrea, Ana Julia (Rip), Barry, Bobby, Burt, Chabelin, Charles, Danny, Elisa, German, Janet, Jose, Maria Elena, Mark, MaryAnn (Rip), Mitch and Steve, you've been INSANELY AWESOME! All the way through.

A special thanks must be given to Daniel Dorse for his magnificent rendering of each of The Equilibrist's Audiobooks. I know, value, and respect the amount of effort and passion you put on these set of precious artful crafts of the spoken word. Thank You!

The next series to follow delves into my life growing up under the loving care and tutelage of my adoptive parents. Erasmus Sr. and Victoria. In particular, it encompasses four different adventures that took place during the many travels we made around the world. In these books I take center stage as the protagonist. The first volume of the series is called: The Orloj of Prague.

See you soon,

Erasmus Cromwell-smith II.

Poetry in Equilibrium

Index

- Note by the Author ...5
- The Quibbler and The Street Juggler ... 7
- The Equilibrist ... 9
- The Balloon Salesman ... 11
- The Boy in The Picture ... 14
- The Gift of Life ... 16
- The Unwavering, Unflickering, Tiny Little Flame ...17
- The Magic in Life ...18
- The Blue Unicorn ... 21
- A Song in The Rain ... 22
- Way, Way, Up There ... 23
- A Strong Group of Few ... 24
- The Land of The Happy People ... 25
- The Spinning Wheel of Life ... 27
- Hope ...29
- An Inspired Life ... 32

Poetry in Equilibrium

- The Past and The Future ... 35

- Reach Out ... 36

- Winning Is Not for The Faint of Heart ...38

- Self-Reliance ... 42

- The Better Instincts of The Heart ... 44

- Life Is Bliss
  (The Importance of The Small Details in Life) ...46

- Love's Rabbit Hole ...48

- The Secret Lies in Opposite Ends at Work Forever ... 50

- What Is Love? ...55

- What Is True Love? ...56

- The Three-Legged Stool ... 60

- Sorting Out the Rest ... 61

- If I Could Only Find You Out There ... 62

- A Labor of Love ...63

- There Is a Life to Be Lived Out There ...65

- Life's True Success Is Being Happy ...68

- The Happiness Formula ... 72

Poetry in Equilibrium

- Optimism ... 75
- Small Sacrifices ... 78
- Of Fate and Fairy Tales ... 80
- My Radiant Goddess of The Night ... 82
- There Is Something About You ... 83
- Life, Character, and Virtue ... 84
- Snap (Snap Out of It) ... 86
- The Chimney Sweep ... 88
- Faith ... 89
- Whispering at Your Heart ... 92
- Life, Evolution and Change ... 94
- Life Wizards ... 97
- Life as a Journey ... 100
- Of Wealth, Fame, and Love ... 105
- Of family True Friendship and Love ... 109
- One Verse at Poet's Row ... 113
- Life as A Circus ... 114
- Those Shiny Curls of Mine ... 118

Poetry in Equilibrium

- Clarity in Life ... 120
- Contemplating Your Face ... 123
- Gratitude ... 127
- Always There ... 130
- A Good Riddle ... 131
- Doubt ... 132
- Duality ... 134
- Geniality ... 137
- Adversity ... 141
- How Is It That You Make Me Feel So Special5 ... 146
- Coherence ... 147
- Virtue ... 149
- Forgiveness ... 151
- Silence Within the Music ... 155
- Reciprocity ... 156
- Defiance ... 159
- Curiosity ... 161
- Decisions ... 163

Poetry in Equilibrium

- Resilience ... 166

- Life, Beauty, and Art ... 168

- What an Amazing Day This Is! ... 174

- Serenity, Courage & Wisdom ... 180

- The Fable of The Old Young Man and The Jester (Fable) ... 183

- A Very Particular Symbiosis ... 190

- The Case of The Curious Child and The Restless Magician (Fable) ... 191

- By the Hand of The Scribbler ... 194

- What an Amazing Blessing Being Together is ... 195

- As to How Love Brightens Everything ... 197

- When I Write to You ... 198

- Convergence ... 200

- It Is Commonly Said That Love Is... ... 201

- When We Are Not Together ... 203

- The Soul's Whispers ... 205

- Animo, Animus, Anima ... 207

- As Time Passes By ... 209

- Do You Remember Those Eyes5 ... 210

Poetry in Equilibrium

- For Our Children ... 211

- Destiny ... 213

- Life Endless Virtuous Circles ... 214

- Enthusiasm ... 216

- Love and Success ... 218

- Joy ... 219

- No Longer Just a Dream (Play) ... 223

- Author's commentary ... 229

- Parting Words by The Author ... 257

Poetry in Equilibrium

Poetry in Equilibrium
was printed in 2022
by RCHC LLC in USA

ЭP

Notes On Poems:

Poetry in Equilibrium

Notes On Poems:

Notes On Poems:

Poetry in Equilibrium

Notes On Poems:

Notes On Poems:

Poetry in Equilibrium

Notes On Poems:

Notes On Poems:

Poetry in Equilibrium

Notes On Poems:

Notes On Poems:

Poetry in Equilibrium

Notes On Poems:

Notes On Poems:

Poetry in Equilibrium

Notes On Poems:

Notes On Poems:

Poetry in Equilibrium

Notes On Poems:

Notes On Poems:

www.ingramcontent.com/pod-product-compliance
Lightning Source LLC
LaVergne TN
LVHW040614250326
834688LV00035B/549